'You're turnin[illegible] a good little sec[illegible]t I'd hear mys[illegible]y can get tire[illegible]s sticking the [illegible] files in the cabinets and typing at a snail's pace.'

Tessa was in no mood to indulge him. From what she had seen, he was far too indulged already. He had been indulged at birth, by being blessed with staggering good looks, and from that it had probably only been a matter of time before self-assurance and charm stepped into the equation. Add a brilliant mind, and the world, she reckoned, had probably been his oyster from when he was a toddler. 'Will that be all?'

'You've gone prune-mouthed on me again. Like a schoolteacher inspecting a particularly offensive pupil.'

'If you don't like my demeanour, then perhaps you'd like me to go?'

'Now you're offended.' He swept out of the chair and was standing by her before she had time to beat a tactical retreat. His voice was gushingly solicitous. 'And I like your demeanour!' He placed his hands on her shoulders and Tessa felt a peculiar surge of heat race though her, sending her heart into furious overdrive.

Cathy Williams is originally from Trinidad, but has lived in England for a number of years. She currently has a house in Warwickshire, which she shares with her husband Richard, her three daughters Charlotte, Olivia and Emma, and their pet cat Salem. She adores writing romantic fiction, and would love one of her girls to become a writer although at the moment she is happy enough if they do their homework and agree not to bicker with one another.

Recent titles by the same author:

THE ITALIAN TYCOON'S MISTRESS
HIS VIRGIN SECRETARY
THE GREEK TYCOON'S SECRET CHILD
HIS CONVENIENT MISTRESS

THE BILLIONAIRE BOSS'S BRIDE

BY
CATHY WILLIAMS

First published in Great Britain 2004
Paperback edition 2005
Harlequin Mills & Boon Limited,
Eton House, 18-24 Paradise Road, Richmond, Surrey TW9 1SR

ISBN 0 263 84115 4

Set in Times Roman 10½ on 12 pt.
01-0105-54410

Printed and bound in Spain
by Litografia Rosés, S.A., Barcelona

CHAPTER ONE

THIS, the first day of Tessa Wilson's new job, was not proving to be a very good day. She stood at the reception desk in the foyer of the avant-garde glasshouse that housed the computer software group for whom she was now working on a super, quite unbelievably bumper salary, and frowned at the chap smiling at her. His badge said that he was called George Grafton and he looked like a George. Plump, balding, comfortable. Tessa's first job had been with a George. They could have been brothers.

'What do you mean you saw them all leaving the building this morning?' Tessa looked at her watch. It was a sensible Casio watch. No frills, no calendar indicating day, month and year, no option to see what time it was in all major cities across the world or to time herself should she spontaneously decide to do a spot of exercise. It was as practical as she was. Practical, diligent and *punctual*.

'And it's eight-thirty in the morning! Surely...'

'You'd think so.' The man at Reception nodded sagely, reading her mind. 'Most people are buzzing in to start the week, but...' He raised his shoulders in an expressive gesture of incomprehension.

Tessa glanced around. Yes, people were pouring into the squat five-storeyed building, which was cunningly designed like Lego bricks surrounding an inner courtyard with benches and eating areas on most of the ground floor. Busy, industrious people who worked for the other companies there. Meanwhile, she was to believe that everyone working for the Diaz Hiscock group had mysteriously decided to take a day off for no apparent reason. It didn't make sense. She wondered nervously whether this was some sort of test, some kind of trick initiation procedure that she was required to get through.

'I'm sorry. This is my first day here. Look. See for yourself.' She pulled out her letter of employment and pointed to the date she was supposed to commence work.

'Yep. You've come on the right day, all right.' Now the man was looking sympathetic, as though she were the recipient of some brutally bad news. 'Can't explain it. I mean, you can go up to the floor and have a look for yourself, but I was here at six and they were streaming out of the building.'

'Maybe they all went out for breakfast,' Tessa said hopefully. That, in itself, was a ludicrous notion. What sort of company operated along the lines of mass desertion at the start of a busy working day, by employees who needed to have breakfast when they surely would have only just arrived?

'Third floor.' He nodded over to where three lifts were furiously trying to deliver employees to their various destinations and reached to answer the telephone.

Tessa dubiously looked at the suited crowd and wiped her sweaty palms on her skirt. She had been full of enthusiasm when she had got out of bed at seven. A little nervous, sure, but she was an experienced PA and confident that she could handle whatever was thrown at her.

Now she wasn't too sure. Now, it occurred to her that the whole interviewing process had been a little on the odd side.

Yes, Diaz Hiscock was a family company, a small but successful and powerful family company, but hadn't it been a little strange that her interview for the job had been with the boss's *mother*? And conducted in the elegant sitting room of a house, over scones and tea? Six weeks ago, Tessa had found it very charming and such a blessed relief from the frantic pace of her old firm. Now she just wondered whether she was dealing with lunatics and had made a fatal error in jacking in her ordinary but perfectly secure job working for an accountancy firm.

'I suppose I'd better... Well!' She neatly folded up her letter and stuffed it back into her handbag. 'Thanks for your help!' She extended one polite hand and smiled. 'And I guess I'll be seeing you around!'

'If not in ten minutes!' He grinned with his hand over the receiver and she smiled weakly back.

'Ha, ha.' If that was meant to sound reassuring then she sincerely hoped that George never decided to go into counselling.

Her face was burning as she waited by the lift, sneaking in when the doors opened and maintaining zero eye contact with anyone else in it, focusing one hundred per cent on the gradual ascent of the lift to the third floor. She wondered whether there would be a roar of laughter behind her when she stepped out onto the third floor, whether they all knew that floor three was vacant.

Roar of laughter, no. Vacant floor, yes. Just as George had predicted. It wasn't a huge office. Reception desk, empty. Tastefully arranged desks with occasional partitions filled the space behind the reception desk. All empty. And as Tessa made her way along the corridor, her feet making no sound as they sunk into the thick pile coffee-coloured carpet, she could feel her heart sinking. Offices to the left and the right, empty. Spacious offices, some with several plasma-screen computer terminals, offices that emanated financial well being, all deserted. The lighting wasn't on and the bleak winter sunshine struggled to make its way through the glass and into the uninhabited office.

She felt like an intruder, but she switched the lights on and they buzzed into fluorescent life. Why the outer door hadn't been locked, she had no idea. Anyone could enter, provided they could get past George. She cleared her throat, meaningfully and noisily, and ventured a tentative, 'Hello.'

The silence that greeted this was deafening.

'You'll find my son a very interesting man to work for,' Mrs Diaz had assured her, sitting back in her high-backed chair and folding her hands elegantly on her lap.

By *interesting* Tessa had assumed willing to give her responsibility. That had been one of the downsides of her last job. She'd done a lot and she'd been respected for what she'd done, but the chances to broaden her horizons hadn't been there. She had heard the adjective *interesting* and been immediately captivated by the prospects it had promised.

Well, day one was proving to be very interesting indeed, if you could call walking around in a ghost office, wearing a suit, interesting.

'Poor Curtis hasn't had much luck with secretaries ever since Nancy quit to live in Australia with her husband.' Mrs Diaz had shaken her head sorrowfully while Tessa had waited for her to expand. Somehow Mrs Diaz was not the sort of lady to interrupt with a barrage of questions. 'He's had a series of doodle heads, little glamour pusses fluttering around and batting their eyelashes. Quite, quite unsuitable for the job of working for my son.'

From the looks of it, anyone would have been quite, quite unsuitable for working for a man who shut up shop at six on a Monday morning, when his new secretary was supposed to arrive that day.

Tessa reluctantly proceeded down the corridor, glancing into the various rooms, increasingly aware that she wasn't going to find any signs of life. It left her in the awkward position of either leaving and risking not being around if everyone in the office reappeared as mysteriously as they seemed to have vanished, or else sitting around in ghost town central twiddling her thumbs until her official going home time of five-thirty.

She was frantically trying to rack up the pros and cons afforded by going or staying when she heard it. A sound. Coming from the office at the very end of the corridor. She picked up speed and walked towards the noise, making sure to check all offices *en route* just in case.

The plaque on the door indicated Curtis Diaz's office. It was slightly ajar. She pushed it open, stepped through into a smaller outside room, through which was a much bigger office, and this time the winter sun was making no headway because thick cream velvet curtains were resolutely closed across the sprawling bank of windows.

Tessa's eyes adjusted to the gloom and she immediately saw the reason for the closed curtains.

Stretched out on a sofa against one side of the wall was a man, lying flat on his back, one arm flung behind him, the other resting contentedly on his stomach. The soft noise that had drawn her attention was simply the sound of his intermittent snoring. In the middle of her appalled inspection, the man cleared his throat and turned onto his side, scaring her witless in the process.

He was wearing a pair of jeans and a long-sleeved rugby-style shirt. Tessa tiptoed towards him and the view expanded into a swarthy face with a hint of stubble darkening his chin. Rumpled black hair completed the picture. Tessa stared, heart thumping, calming herself with the knowledge that at least she wasn't in the building alone. She might have stepped into the twilight zone on the third floor, but all the other floors were teeming with people and good old George was only a phone call away.

She stepped briskly past the inert figure on the couch, reached for the cord by the wall and pulled.

'Okay, buster! Who are you and what are you doing in this office?'

The man struggled awake, groaning, and then subsided back, this time with one of the cushions covering his face.

Tessa walked towards him, gazed at the rumpled sight with distaste, and yanked the cushion straight out from beneath his arm, and this time it worked. Gratified, she watched as the bum blearily hoisted himself into a semi-sitting position and focused on where she was standing with her hands pinned to her hips and her mouth narrowed into a line of uncompromising severity.

'I don't know how you got into this office, buddy…' Of course she knew! Hadn't it been wide open to whoever might choose to enter? Hadn't she herself wondered at the utter lack of basic security? 'But you can get right out! This isn't a doss house for any passing vagrant who decides to come in for a quick kip!'

'Wha…?'

'Oh, yes, you heard me!' Tessa could feel herself well and truly on a roll now. First, she had showed up, *on time* and dressed in a spanking new suit, ready to make a good impression on day one, only to find herself wandering through an empty office like a fool, and as if that wasn't enough here she was, confronted by a supine figure snoring away merrily, probably sleeping off a hangover from whatever bottle of methylated spirits he had downed the night before outside the building.

'Look at you!' she snapped, leaning forward and wrinkling her nose as the apparition pushed himself into a more upright sitting position so that he could look at her in perplexed astonishment. 'You should be ashamed of yourself!'

'I should?'

'You most certainly should! An able-bodied young man like yourself, sneaking into an unoccupied office and just *going to sleep*! Don't tell me you can't get out there and find yourself a job!' The able-bodied young man was staring at her in a way that was beginning to make her feel very self-conscious. He was also, now that she could see him properly, an extremely good looking specimen, underneath the scruffy demeanour. His face was darkly handsome, in a tough, rugged sort of way, a compelling face that made her breath catch in her throat for a second or two. Tessa got a grip of herself and glared.

'I'm afraid I'm going to have to report you,' she said quietly, while narrowed blue eyes began to gleam with amusement. 'And you won't find that very funny! Have your fun and grin away, but when the police come and you're thrown into some cell *downtown*, you *won't be grinning*!'

'Cell downtown?' He couldn't help himself. His lips twitched and he grinned with wicked amusement. 'This isn't New York, this is London. I think you've been watching too many American police shows.' He raked his fingers through his hair and reluctantly stood up.

Disconcerted, Tessa took a couple of steps backwards. The man, who was now massaging the back of his neck with his hand and glancing round the office in an offhand way, was very tall. Very tall, with a solid muscularity that was a bit alarming.

'Maybe I have,' she said placatingly. She watched warily as the man ambled over to the window and peered out.

'What time is it, anyway?'

'A little after half past eight.'

That met with a grunt. 'No wonder I feel like something the cat brought in,' he muttered, swinging round to face her.

'I'm going to have to call George...' Tessa began. He had made her feel like a melodramatic idiot for having mentioned police and cells. George would have to deal with this. It wasn't part of her job—secretary and makeshift security guard for premises that should have been locked in the first place.

'Who are you, anyway?'

'Who am *I*?' Tessa regarded the man with amazement. 'Let's just say that I'm the person who found you comatose on a sofa, *trespassing, from all accounts*.'

'Yes, but do you have a name?' He plonked himself down on the leather swivel chair at the desk and she gaped incredulously at the sheer nerve. 'Oh, God. No. Skip that question. It's coming to me now. I know who you are.' He pushed the chair back just far enough to enable him to stretch his legs out onto the desk, then he folded his hands behind his head and proceeded to look at her with a highly amused, alert expression.

'Do you? You mean you're a trespasser *as well as* being a clairvoyant? I'm impressed! I'm not too sure whether George will be—'

'You're Miss Wilson.' He grinned but with the ground rapidly shifting underneath her feet, grinning back was the last thing Tessa felt inclined to do. 'Have a seat. Really. You look as though you might just fall down if you don't.'

'I think I need to call George...' she said uncertainly, sitting down.

'You don't. Well, you *can* if you really feel you need to, but believe me, that'll just lead to embarrassment. Yours. Look, let me put you out of your misery and introduce myself...' He stood up, all formality now, even though the impression was hijacked by the casualness of his clothes. 'I'm Curtis Diaz.' He stretched out his hand and smiled with sickening kindness.

'You…you can't be…' Tessa ignored the outstretched hand and grasped the handbag on her lap tightly.

Well, she *had* been bored with the monotonous tedium of her last job! What better antidote than to be thrust into a surreal world where she didn't have a clue as to what was going on?

'Why not?'

'Because…'

'I know.' He looked ruefully down at himself and shook his head. 'Code of dress, right? Powerful men who run powerful companies dress in pinstriped suits and ties, always carefully knotted at the neck.'

Tongue-tied and mortified, Tessa stared back at him, her mouth half open and a delicate bloom of colour rising up her cheeks. She wasn't fashioned to deal with situations like these. Above all things, Tessa Wilson liked to be in control. Time and time again she had seen people passively and helplessly steamrollered by events. It happened in their jobs, it happened with their love lives. She often wondered what would have happened to her and Lucy if she had been like all those people who never seemed to cater for the unforeseen.

The unforeseen had happened with her and she had dealt with it, and had continued dealing with life by reining it in. She liked to know where she was going and how she was going to get there because working things out, knowing where she stood, made her feel safe.

She also resented the fact that he was laughing at her.

'I don't know what's going on,' she said stiffly. Her body was ramrod straight in the chair.

'And I apologise. Profusely.' He levered himself back into his chair and reclined back. 'Allow me to explain. My team and I have just completed a weekend of virtual solid work, thrashing a deal out with one of our suppliers and then finalising the nitty-gritty with the lawyers. We didn't finish until the early hours of the morning at which point I decided to let them all go home and catch up on some well-deserved rest.'

So this was what his mother had meant by interesting, Tessa thought dazedly. When she had used that word, Tessa had tied it up in her head with the job and not the man. The man, she was slowly realising, was nothing like she had expected. She had expected someone a bit like Mrs Diaz. Sophisticated, very English and probably fair haired. The man staring at her, waiting for her to digest his information, couldn't have been further from her expectations. Restless, passionate energy vibrated out of him in waves and the only bit of him that resembled his mother were his eyes, which were as blue and as piercing, except a lot more dramatic against his olive colouring and dark, springy hair.

'Right. Well, I wish you had telephoned me to explain that my services wouldn't be required today…'

'Never occurred to me,' Curtis informed her truthfully. He idly switched on one of the two computer terminals on his desk and it buzzed into life with a faint humming sound.

Poor woman, he thought, glancing across at the rigid pink-faced figure sitting opposite him. He really should have stood firm and recruited his own secretary, but he loved his mother dearly and giving in had eventually seemed preferable to staging a protracted war. Mothers liked to think they knew best and his mother was no exception to the rule. She had stared at him gimlet-eyed and told him in no uncertain terms that hiring floozies, as she had called them, was a waste of company money.

'But they look good,' he had protested, thinking back to the last one, a red-haired, buxom wench who had worn delightful handkerchiefs, which she had loosely claimed were miniskirts.

'Which is hardly a satisfactory recommendation when it comes to being a secretary.'

The tirade had gone on and on until he had thrown up his hands in resignation and left it to her to sort out.

Unfortunately, looking at the Tessa character now, he could immediately see the downsides of his mother's well-intentioned but misguided rationale.

The poor girl looked as though she had suddenly found herself wandering in the vicinity of hell without any map giving her the quickest route back to normality. He sighed under his breath and raked his fingers through his hair.

'Look, Miss Wilson…now that you're here, maybe we should go and grab some breakfast, have a bit of a chat…'

'Some breakfast…?'

'That's right,' Curtis said, curbing his irritation, 'I haven't eaten since yesterday…some time…' He stood up and stretched, eyeing her out of the corner of his eye, which only confirmed his opinion that she was not going to be suitable for the job.

'I'm hungry,' he told her bluntly, throwing on his overcoat. 'I need something to eat and dried-up slices of pizza in the bin just isn't going to do it for me. And we need to have a little talk.'

Tessa scrambled to her feet and hurried after him as he headed out of his office. It took quite some running. High-heeled shoes might look the part but when it came to scurrying after someone who walked at a pace that most people ran, they weren't exactly practical. She nearly careered into him when he finally came to a dead stop by the lift.

'So,' he began conversationally, noticing the way she had edged away from him in the confines of the lift, back pressed against the side as though her life depended on it, 'it must have been a bit of a shock when you came to work this morning and found the offices empty…?'

'I was a little surprised.'

'Hmm. A little surprised. Diplomatic choice of words.'

'George at Reception had warned me that he had witnessed a mass exodus earlier in the morning, but, naturally, I thought that he might have exaggerated a bit. I…well, I wasn't prepared for…'

'A scene from a late-night horror movie?' The lift doors disgorged them back into the expansive waiting area where George was still in attendance. He winked at her and exchanged a large grin with Curtis.

'So you managed to find one still alive and kicking, then?'

'Don't tease her, George. She's had a very stressful day so far.'

The banter made Tessa feel suddenly foolish and sidelined and the unfortunate butt of some ongoing joke at her expense. 'I wouldn't say *stressful*,' she retorted, 'just a little *disorienting*.'

She felt the warm pressure of his fingers on her elbow as he led her towards the revolving door and heard the deep throb of his laughter, which brought on an attack of unwarranted confusion.

'Okay. Disorienting. Are you going to be warm enough out here with just a suit? The café's not far but it's still a walk…'

'I'm fine.' She resisted the temptation to add that she would have brought her coat if she had foreseen a day that involved walking. But, on day one, she had decided to treat herself to a taxi both ways and had not envisaged needing anything heavier than her cream-and-black-flecked woollen suit.

'I don't suppose your last job involved too many episodes of *disorientation*?'

'Most jobs don't.' Their destination was within sight.

Literally a good, old-fashioned café with no trimmings. It was heaving, with an eclectic mix of suited businessmen, rough-and-ready workmen, taxi drivers and women who looked as though they had spent the night on the tiles and were on their way home. Most, though, were taking their breakfasts away with them and it was a relief to be out of the cold and in the warmth.

'Do you come here often?' Tessa heard herself ask inanely.

'Does a good breakfast. Now, what will you have?' He positioned her at one of the tables and narrowed his eyes to read the blackboard with the specials, which was behind her.

'Coffee.'

'Right. Wait here.' Within ten minutes he was back carrying a tray on which were two steaming mugs of coffee and a plate mountainously piled with bacon, egg, black pudding and what looked suspiciously like fried bread.

Oh, your arteries are really going to thank you for that injection of cholesterol, she was tempted to say.

'Don't even think of saying what's going through your head.'

'I wasn't thinking anything!'

'Tell me about your last job,' was all he replied, leaving her to wonder uncomfortably how he had managed to read her mind.

'I told your mother...well, it's all there on my CV.' Comprehension filtered through. 'But I guess you didn't read my CV.'

'I left the finer details of your employment to my mother. Your last job?'

Tessa sipped her coffee, which was surprisingly aromatic. 'I worked for a firm of accountants. Not one of the top three, but one of the bigger ones, doing all the usual stuff. I'm fully computer literate and can handle pretty much anything from spreadsheets to invoicing.' Silence followed that, interrupted only by his eating. 'I've also arranged training courses, overseen meetings, in short done everything a PA is trained to do.'

Curtis washed down the last of his breakfast with a generous mouthful of coffee, then sat back in his chair and looked at her assessingly.

'And you enjoyed it, did you?'

'Well, yes, of course. I was there for a number of years—'

'Why the change of job, in that case?'

Gone was the light-hearted, unconventional man who had confronted her at eight-thirty that morning. In its place was someone shrewd and forthright and very focused.

'It wasn't going anywhere.' Tessa flinched away from that disconcerting blue gaze. 'I felt that I needed to expand my horizons and, in a company like that, it's only possible if you're one of the professionals.'

'But you liked working there, aside from the obvious limitations, am I right?' He watched as she nodded and could hear her wondering where this was going. 'You liked the order, the environment, the routine.'

'Those things are very important, I think, in the successful running of a company,' Tessa said defensively.

Order. Routine. Yes, she did like those things. They formed the perimeter of her life and always had. How else would she have been able to cope with bringing up her unruly ten-year-old sister when she had only been going on eighteen herself? In fact, compared to Lucy, or maybe because of her, she, Tessa, had always had her head firmly screwed on. Her parents had always praised her for that. Lucy might be the beauty with the ebullience, but Tessa was the responsible one, the one on whom they relied. The one on whom they had still been relying when their car had swerved into a tree on a rainy night back home. Tessa had mourned and grieved and picked up the pieces the best she could and, yes, had fallen back on order and routine to help her through.

She blinked away the sudden intrusion of her past and, when she looked at him, she found him staring at her, his bright blue eyes narrowed on her face.

'Don't you agree with me?' The way he looked at her made her feel hot and bothered, even though he didn't seem to be looking at her in a critical way. Perhaps it was the level of containment, at odds with the aggressively confident and outgoing exterior. Here was a man, she suspected, who did precisely as he liked and yet remained a closed book. It was nerve-racking. 'I mean, you run a successful company. Surely you don't just jump in a haphazard manner from one day to the next, hoping for the best and keeping your fingers crossed?'

Curtis threw back his head and laughed. 'No. Not quite. That approach doesn't often work, although it sounds as though it could be quite a lot of fun.'

Tessa shuddered. *Fun?* Never knowing from one minute to the next what life was going to throw at you? Not a chance.

'You don't agree? Well, never mind. So you've worked in your last job for…how many years?'

'Nine, give or take a few months,' she said uncomfortably.

Curtis gave a low whistle under his breath.

'And you are…? Age…?'

'Twenty-eight.'

'At work at nineteen and then staying put with the same company…'

'Which should tell you how experienced I am.' Why did

she have the sinking feeling that this was the interview that should have been conducted from the start? 'I'm sorry. I thought I *had* the job. I thought your mother was in a position to offer it to me.' She could feel herself perspiring under her armpits and she wished she had removed her jacket when she had first sat down, just as he had done with his overcoat. He looked as comfortable as a cat on a feather quilt while she felt rattled, uneasy and hot.

'Oh, of course she was.' He shrugged. 'It's a family firm. I run it completely, take full responsibility for all profits and losses, but my brother and my mother are naturally still interested in what's going on, and occasionally my mother will offer her input. In the matter of my hiring someone to work for me, she insisted, and I expect she told you why.'

'She mentioned that some of your secretaries in the past had been a bit…unsuitable.'

'Except I don't imagine she was quite so restrained in her description.'

Tessa frowned and tucked her hair neatly behind her ears. She had fine, slippery, very smooth shoulder-length auburn hair that had a tendency to slide forward and brush her face if she wasn't careful about tying it back. Today, on Lucy's advice, she had decided to wear it loose so that she wouldn't look like a schoolmarm on her first day out. Now, she was regretting the impulse because for some reason she felt as though she needed the protection of her normally very restrained look.

'I'll bet she referred to them as *bimbos*,' Curtis added helpfully as Tessa was struggling to come up with a diplomatic way of paraphrasing what had been said to her.

'The thing is…' He leaned forward and rested his arms on the table. He had pushed up the sleeves of his jumper and she noticed that he had very strong forearms, dusted with black hair. He, too, wore a simple watch although his looked crashingly expensive, unlike hers. 'Bimbos suited me. How can I explain this?'

Tessa's heart went into freefall at that rhetorical question.

'I don't work in an environment that's anything like the one you have spent the last nine years, give or take a month or so, enjoying. The world of computers and computer software is far more about creativity and vibrancy and foresight than the world of accountants. The bimbos might have been a little lax when it came to typing and shorthand but they knew how to work around me.'

'Your mother said the last one was only there for a matter of six weeks.'

'Ah. Fifi *did* have a spot of bother now and again with some of the basics...'

'Fifi?' Two spots of angry colour blazed on her cheeks and she leaned forward into him, clutching the mug with both her hands. 'Are you telling me that I'm too dull to work for you because I'm good at what I do and don't fill all the physical attributes you think are necessary to a good secretary?'

'I'm telling you that what I don't want is someone addicted to schedules who is incapable of going with the flow. That would be unfair on me and even more unfair on you. Obviously, I would give you healthy compensation for the inconvenience caused.'

'Inconvenience?' Calm and control flew out of the window at the speed of light. Tessa inhaled deeply in an attempt to retrieve some of it. 'I have thrown in a perfectly good job in order to take up this one. I simply cannot afford to be tossed out onto the streets like a...a *beggar* gatecrashing a private party to scour the employment agencies looking for something else!'

'A beggar gatecrashing a private party...?' Curtis sat back and gave her his full attention. The peak breakfast-hour rush was over and the café was now relatively quiet, with only one other table occupied and stragglers coming in for their daily tea and bacon butties.

'This isn't funny!'

'No, it's not. And, like I said, you won't walk away empty-handed. A highly qualified girl like you should have no difficulty finding another position in a company that would suit your talents a lot more.'

'And how do you know what would suit my talents when you aren't even prepared to give me a chance?' The horrendous unfairness of it sent a streak of molten fire racing through her. 'I have bills to settle, Mr Diaz! Food to buy, rent to pay and a sister to finish supporting!'

'You support your sister?'

'At art college. She has one more year there.'

Curtis sighed and made his mind up. Three months' probation. He owed it to his mother, after all, and if the girl didn't work out, then at least he had given it a go. He would give her vital but background jobs to do and would just have to make sure that she didn't compromise the vibrancy of his company, which had gone some way to catapulting it from obscure newcomer to innovative front runner.

'Okay. Three months' probation, then we can take it from there…'

Tessa breathed a sigh of relief. Three months would give her a bit of time to look for something else and the pay was so fabulous that she would be able to put aside a healthy amount of money in that space of time. Because the bottom line was that the man was right. She needed to work for someone organised, someone more *grounded*, someone less flamboyant who didn't make her stammer like a schoolgirl every time he fixed those vivid blue eyes on her. And, whatever his mother had said, he needed someone to look good and to slot in. He needed another Fifi.

CHAPTER TWO

'OKAY! Where the hell have you put that file?'

Curtis stormed out of his office and proceeded to circle her desk until he was standing squarely in front of her, and, as if that weren't enough, he then leaned forward, planting both hands on her desk until Tessa was reluctantly forced to acknowledge him.

The past two weeks had been a learning curve. Curtis Diaz was brilliant, forceful, outspoken, alarming and utterly unpredictable. He obeyed none of the rules most bosses observed. The first in-house meeting she had gone to had been an experience that had left her feeling dazed for hours afterwards. Ideas had bounced around the room like bullets, voices had been raised and anything suggested that had failed to take into account probable loopholes had been loudly shouted down without any attempt made to soothe nerves or compromise.

Interestingly, none of the staff had seemed disconcerted by their boss's unconventional approach to company management.

'Well?' Curtis roared. 'Have you gone deaf? Is there life in there?'

'There's no need to shout,' Tessa said quietly, but she was adjusting fast to his displays of temper. Rule one, she had learned, was not to automatically cringe back. To start with, she had wondered how his Fifis had coped with his overpowering personality. Then it occurred to her that he had probably never raised his voice in their presence. They were there for his visual satisfaction and, as she had discovered, most of the intricate work had been done by one of the other secretaries out of loyalty to their charismatic leader. The various strings of Fifis had filed, brought cups of coffee and brightened up his office. She, on the other hand, not having the glamour looks to fall back on, was treated like everyone else.

'I am not shouting,' he growled now, thrusting his dark face further forward. 'I'm asking a perfectly reasonable question.'

'Oh, right. Well, thanks for pointing that out. My mistake.' Tessa said that with such understated calm that he made an unintelligible sound under his breath and drew back.

'I gave the file to Richard yesterday before I left. He wanted to go over some of the costings again.'

'Well, you'd better go and fetch it.' He prowled off to stand by the window, hands stuffed into his pockets.

'Anything else while I'm there?' Tessa stood up and looked at him. She might be getting used to the way he operated, but she doubted in the three-month target she had set herself that she would ever become used to the way he looked. He was quite simply overwhelming. When he banged around the office or called her in so that he could dictate something to her in that rapid-fire manner of his, she was fine, but every time he focused his attention fully on her, as he was doing now, she could feel every nerve in her body begin to quiver with clammy, restless awareness.

'No.' Blue eyes did a frowning, absent-minded inspection of her and returned to her face, which had pinkened. 'Just get the file and come into my office with it. There are one or two things I want to discuss with you. Oh, you might as well grab us both a cup of coffee while you're about it, even though you're not much use on the coffee-making front.' That little jab seemed to do the trick of snapping him out of his mood because he grinned at her. 'Now, I bet you're going to tell me that a highly qualified PA isn't responsible for making decent coffee for her boss.'

Tessa took a deep breath and counted to ten. He didn't often tease her and, when he did, it always sent a tingle of unwanted emotion racing through her. The only way she knew how to handle that was to be as bland and literal as possible, so she gave him a perplexed look as though considering his criticism fully at face value.

'You haven't complained about my coffee-making skills before.'

'Too weak. Weak coffee is for weak men.'

This time her finely arched eyebrows flew up in an expression of amused disbelief.

'Oh, really? I never realised that before.'

'Didn't think so. Aren't you glad that you're learning such amazing things every day, thanks to me?'

'Oh, absolutely,' she murmured, looking down and sliding away from her desk. 'I really don't know how I survived in my last job before.'

She could almost *hear* him grinning as she swept out of the room and headed to Richard's office.

Three days after she had started, his mother had telephoned her at the office to find out how she was enjoying working for her son.

'It's a unique experience,' Tessa had confided truthfully. 'I've never worked for anyone like your son before.'

'I hope you're managing to keep him in order,' Mrs Diaz had said. 'He can be a little intimidating to the uninitiated. Runs rings around people.'

'Well, he doesn't intimidate me,' she had replied without pausing for breath.

Well, he did, though not in the way his mother had implied. She was confident in her abilities to do her job to the highest standard, thereby giving him no chance to slam into her for inefficiency, but on the personal level it was a different question altogether. He had a certain magnetism that made her quail inside and it was a source of abundant relief to her that she could school her expressions so that that particular weakness was never exposed.

He was waiting for her in his office when she returned ten minutes later with the file and a cup of coffee that was so strong that she could almost have stood the teaspoon upright in it.

He had pushed his chair back and pulled out the bottom drawer of the desk, which he was using as an impromptu footrest.

'Pull up a chair,' he said, 'and close the door behind you.'

'Close the door?'

'That's right. No need to repeat everything I say parrot-style.'

Tessa didn't say anything. She shut his door, handed him the file and then sat down with her notepad on her lap and her hand poised to take down whatever he was about to dictate.

'So,' he began, 'how are you enjoying it here?'

Tessa looked up at him in surprise. 'Fine, thank you.'

'Fine. Hmm.' What he *had* intended to discuss, amongst other things, were the costings of extending IT operations somewhere in the Far East. She might not, he had realised, be the eye candy he had previously employed, but she hadn't been kidding when she had told him that she was good at what she did. Not only were his thoughts channelled into expert documentation, but she could involve herself in more complex debates, which he had discovered was quite a useful talent.

Her persona, though, was a more difficult nut to crack. She greeted everything he said with the same unshakeable composure, which was beginning to prick his curiosity. His method of management was an open-door policy, whereby all his employees were free to voice whatever was on their minds, and they did. Moreover, he had become accustomed to a fast turnover of secretaries who wore their feelings on their sleeves. He liked the people who worked for him to be three-dimensional; he enjoyed the fact that he knew about their personal lives as well as their professional ones. It made for a tightly knit team of people who were secure enough in their abilities to take criticism and felt valued enough to dish it out should they see fit.

Tessa, thrown into this volatile, verbal bunch, was an enigma and it was beginning to bother him.

'I'm concerned that you might be finding the pace of this industry a little too swift for you.'

'Would you mind explaining that?' She looked at him with unreadable brown eyes.

Curtis watched her, irritated by the fact that he couldn't get underneath that smooth face of hers to the workings of her mind. He began to tap his propelling pencil softly on the protective leather mat in front of his computer.

'I feel I'm keeping up with the pace of work here,' she interjected, trying and failing to think back of any time over the past fortnight when she had been unable to cope with the lightning speed of his thoughts.

'Oh, I don't deny that.'

'What, then?'

'Being successful at a job is only partly to do with an ability to cope with the workload. Coping doesn't necessarily equate to happiness and happiness goes hand in hand with motivation.'

'There's no need for you to be concerned with my happiness,' Tessa told him. 'If I was unhappy, I would quit.'

Having not meant to bring this topic up at all, Curtis now found himself uncomfortably aware that he wanted to prolong it until she said something personal rather than simply showing him the same face of complete composure that she had shown ever since she had first started.

'Why? Have other people been complaining about me?'

'Oh, no. On the contrary. I've been told in no uncertain terms that it was high time I hired someone a little more down-to-earth than my usual brand of secretary.'

What woman in her right mind would like being described as *down-to-earth*? Tessa wondered. Especially when the description came from someone who looked the way this man did? Today, in deference to a board meeting that had been held with some particularly crusty clients, he had toned his dress code down a notch. Even so, the pink-and-white-striped shirt failed to give the impression of a conservative traditionalist, especially as it was twinned with an outrageously patterned, very slender tie, the likes of which she had personally never seen before, leading her to assume that it must be handmade.

'But you don't agree.' The criticism, packaged up like a compliment, hurt more than she liked.

'My theory is that for an employee to really enjoy his or her job, they've got to feel as though they fit in.' He wondered why he was labouring this point and whether it was so important to get to the bottom of her when she was doing her job perfectly well. Better than well, in actual fact.

There was no answer to that. She spoke to everybody, sometimes she even went to lunch with a couple of them, although the workload was so intense that she was happy to eat a sandwich at her desk, a half-hour break before she carried on with what she was doing.

'We're like a family here,' he broke into her thoughts, his voice piously ruminative, 'and, call me old-fashioned, but I like to know what happens in my employees' lives. It makes them feel wanted and it's very important to me that they feel wanted.' He looked at her from under his long, dark lashes and noticed the very slight shift in her position.

'I don't think anyone could call you old-fashioned,' Tessa said, dodging the net he was trying to throw around her.

'No? Why would that be, do you think?'

'Because...because you really don't...you're quite unconventional compared to the other people I've worked for.' That was the understatement of the year, she thought. He was like a peacock amongst sparrows compared to her previous employers, for she had circulated within the firm in which she had worked on a fairly regular basis over the years.

'Hence my unconventional approach to my employees...'

'And you don't mind if they have an unconventional approach to you in return?' Tessa felt quite proud of this neat sleight of hand that had managed to toss the question right back at him.

'Not in the slightest. My personal life is an open book.'

'I'm...I don't believe in bringing my private life to work,' Tessa said, staring down at her fingers. She wondered what he would make of her private life. It was an open book as well, except hers had very little writing in it, at least on the men front, which she was now sure was what was niggling him. 'Perhaps we could discuss these costings?' she prompted tentatively. 'I really need to leave on time tonight and it's almost five-thirty.'

That sparked his curiosity again. What exactly did she

get up to when she left this office? Nothing that relied on her leaving her work promptly, he knew, because over the past two weeks her hours had been anything but regular and not once had she complained.

'Why's that?' he asked idly. 'Hot date?'

Tessa flushed. She could feel herself reddening and it made her more defensive than usual. 'Actually, tonight's hot date is taking place in the supermarket and involves cooking spaghetti Bolognese for four of my friends from my last job as well as Lucy and two of *her* friends.'

'Lucy?'

'My sister.' Blonde, blue-eyed and beautiful. Just the sort of woman that Curtis Diaz would make a beeline for. If she could have yanked back her words, she would have.

'Oh, the one you're putting through college. By the way, how is it that you're responsible for paying for her education?'

'That's just the way it is and it has been that way since I was a teenager.' She shrugged, dismissing his interest and looking down at the redundant pad sitting on her lap.

'Must be a burden on your finances,' he remarked thoughtfully. 'Is that why you took this job? Because of the salary?' His thoughts were already moving along, though, playing with other possibilities and enjoying the probing process while being fully aware that he was prying into areas of her life in which he was unwanted.

'Amongst other things.'

'Oh, sure, job satisfaction.' He linked his fingers behind his head and surveyed her with open curiosity. 'Of course, more money would be reason enough. After all, there's only so much of those free pleasures you can have, especially in winter when it's freezing cold outside. Walks in the park just aren't quite the same, I find… Oh, I forgot. All your money's going to help your little sister through college. You should tell her to take on some evening work so she can put herself through.'

'Lucy isn't into evening work,' Tessa said without thinking. She could have kicked herself. She could almost hear his ears pricking up at that admission. The truth was that she *had* mentioned evening work to Lucy and had hit a brick wall. Her sister liked to party. The small legacy from their parents, which had been shared between them, had been put into storage, on the advice of their very shrewd solicitor who had foreseen a time when it might be needed to buy property. Tessa had had no difficulty in concurring with this as far as her half went. Lucy, after much nagging when she had hit her landmark eighteenth birthday, had agreed to have a small allowance paid into her bank account every month to fund her lifestyle. Tessa should have stood firm, but as always she had caved in. Most people did when faced with Lucy's optimistic, winning smile.

'Not into evening work? You mean she's happy for you to pay for her so that she can enjoy herself?'

'I don't mind.'

'Tut-tut. There's nothing worse than a martyr.'

That did it. Tessa snapped shut her notepad and gave him her steeliest glare. 'I can think of lots of things worse, actually, and I am *not* a martyr. Lucy is much younger than me and she's always been the baby of the family. We all indulged her, including me, and I don't mind at all paying for her fees. She deserves to have a good time while she's young!'

'Because you never did?' he asked quickly, hitting the mark with such effortless ease that Tessa's mouth dropped open and she was momentarily lost for words. 'I mean,' he continued to expand in a lazy, musing voice, 'you were forced into the role of surrogate mother when you were just a teenager and since then you haven't really stopped. Who knows? Maybe you get a personal vicarious thrill from your sister's fun-loving lifestyle because you were denied it.'

'I thought we were going to go through these costings.'

'We are. In a minute. It's just so rewarding finding out more about one of my employees, knowing what makes them tick.'

'You're not *finding out more about me,*' Tessa said coolly, sitting back in her chair. 'You're second-guessing my life.'

'You're not denying any of what I've said.'

'I don't have to. I'm here to do a job. I don't have to defend myself in the process.'

'True.' He sat forward abruptly and gave her a dazzling smile loaded with a mixture of charm and apology. 'And it's outrageous of me to start prying and probing into what's none of my business! I'm glad you spoke your mind and told me to back off!' He absent-mindedly flicked his tie between his fingers and continued to look at her contritely. 'That's the problem, you know. I rush in where I'm not wanted and make a nuisance of myself.'

'It's good you recognise the problem, in that case,' Tessa said weakly. The warmth and sincerity in his voice had punctured all traces of indignation. Now she felt as though *she* should be the one apologising, for what she had no idea!

'Oh, I do!' He shot her a crooked smile that would have had any little old lady buckling at the knees. He was also an incurable flirt. She had seen him in action, taking time to chat with the cleaner who came in after hours, even though she was a happily married lady in her mid fifties. He did it almost without thinking. She wondered how many of his young, pretty secretaries had lost their heads over him. Whatever, she assumed that he was as charming when he dispatched them as he was when he hired them, because in the space of two weeks she had transferred no less than three separate calls from women who said that they had worked for him in the past and were just phoning to touch base.

It was to her credit, she thought now, that she could withstand his personality as successfully as she did. She did so now by sending him a dry look that warned him not to overplay his card and he laughed, reading the message in her brown eyes.

As always, though, when it came to work, he was all concentrated brilliance. She barely noticed the time flying by when, after an hour, his office was occupied by four of the computer whizkids sprawled on the sofa, one perched on his desk, all animatedly discussing ideas for some new software while she sat rapidly making notes and working out in her head their order of priority for when she came to transcribe them the following morning.

She realised the time when Robert Harding, a brilliant computer mind behind thick spectacles and the classic nerd look, stretched and stood up to leave. Then she looked at her watch and gave a little shriek of dismay.

'I have to go!' She stood up, feeling like a traitor because she was leaving work ahead of everyone else, even though five-thirty had come and gone a full forty-five minutes ago.

'Oh, yes, the spaghetti Bolognese!' Curtis grinned and stood up as well, putting an end to the impromptu meeting which, uncharacteristically, met with groans of reluctance.

'Now, now!' he chided them, sauntering over to unhook his bomber jacket from the sleek walnut-fronted cupboard that stored several essential items of clothing just in case he happened to sleep in the office one night. Through the dividing door, he could see Tessa scuttling around her desk, frantically tidying things away. Strands of hair were escaping from her neatly coiffured coil, as if even *they* were in a state of agitation about the lateness of the hour.

'I think we ought to stay on for, let's say, another hour or so, Curtis!' Adam Beesley's youthful face was bright with enthusiasm.

'Remember what they say about all work and no play! You don't want to end up a dullard, do you?' He moved towards his office door, keeping Tessa within his line of vision while he continued to address the assorted crew now reluctantly rising to their feet. 'Fine line, team, between hard-working and sad!' He exited his office to hoots of laughter and followed Tessa to the lift, insinuating himself in front of her just as she was about to press the button.

'I want to apologise for keeping you here so late,' he murmured.

Tessa pressed the button and stared in front of her. 'Normally, I wouldn't mind. I don't like clock-watching but tonight—'

'Yes, the friends, the cooking. Here's where I come in.' At that moment the lift arrived and the doors parted. As soon as they were in the lift, he turned to her and smiled. Maybe it was her imagination, but that full wattage smile in the confines of a lift seemed to be a lot more potent. She felt her skin heat up and the hand she had thrust into her coat pocket curled into a little, nervous fist.

Curtis at work was her boss, even when the man intruded. Curtis out of work was something she didn't think about although unconsciously she must have found the thought disturbing because she had not once taken up any offers to go anywhere for a quick drink with the gang before heading home.

'Since it's my fault your meal's going to be ruined, let me take all of you out to dinner...'

'What?' Her head swung round sharply and for a few

nightmarish seconds she actually struggled for breath while she tried to cope with the horror of his suggestion.

'I said—'

'Yes, I heard what you said! And it's...very...well, considerate of you, but out of the question. Thank you all the same!'

'But you won't have time to prepare your meal...'

'I can whip something else up. No need for you to worry about it.' Panic licked through her and she tried to see his suggestion for what it was, an offbeat but instinctively gracious offer from someone who had kept her working later than intended. Curtis was not a man who was stingy with his gestures. He would think nothing of taking her out along with seven other people for a slap-up meal at some expensive restaurant somewhere.

She realised that her reaction was out of proportion because *she* didn't want him to invade her private life at all, not in any way.

The lift had reached the ground floor and she scooted out, planning to escape into the dark cold outside, thereby putting an end to their conversation.

'So I take it you won't accept my offer...' He reached out and swung her around, leaving his arm curled on her wrist. 'I'm cut to the quick.'

'No, you're not!' Tessa said sharply. His hand was burning through the layers of clothing. She could feel it like a hot brand stamping down into her flesh, making her want to squirm.

'You're right. I'm not. But that's only because I expected you to refuse my offer.'

'You did?'

He nodded gravely and the pressure of his hand lessened, although he didn't remove it and didn't appear to notice her surreptitious attempts to ease it away.

'I did.' He shot her a smug look. 'Isn't it nice the way I can tune in to you after only two weeks?'

Tessa ignored that. 'Well, why did you bother to offer if you knew I was going to refuse?'

'Because I still intend to help you out, whether you like it or not.' Instead of heading towards the revolving door at the front, he swivelled her back round to the lift and pressed the down button. 'I'm going to drive you to your house and, on the way, I'm going to stop off and get a take-away and, before you open your mouth to gently turn my magnanimous offer down, there's no debate.'

She was ushered back into the lift, this time down to the basement, where a handful of people were given the privilege of secured parking. In central London that in itself was worth its weight in gold.

'Slightly selfish reasons here,' he continued, leaning back against the mirrored side of the lift.

'What?' Tessa's voice was apprehensive. Trying to predict this man's moves was like trying to predict the weather from a sealed box underground. Utterly impossible.

'I need you to do me a small favour.'

'Favour? What favour?'

He didn't answer immediately. Instead, as the lift disgorged them into the compact underground car park he led her towards his sleek, low-slung sports car, a shiny black Mercedes that was the last word in breathtaking extravagance and just the sort of car she would have imagined him driving. Not for him the big, safe cars with practical boot space and generous passenger-toting potential!

'One of my babies,' he said, grinning at her and sweeping a loving hand across the gleaming bonnet.

'One of them? You mean you have a fleet of cars lurking away somewhere?' Yes, she could imagine that too. A dozen racy little numbers tucked away somewhere, ready and waiting for when they might be put to use driving his racy female numbers to racy little nightclubs. She scowled in the darkness and wondered how such creative genius could be simultaneously shallow and superficial.

'You snorted.'

'I beg your pardon?' Had she?

'You snorted just then. A very disapproving snort. What's wrong about having a fleet of sports cars? I thought you women liked that sort of thing.'

'Some might.' His amusement was very irritating. She tilted her chin up and stared frostily out of the window.

'But not you.' He slotted a card into the machine at the side and the exit barrier went up.

'That's right,' Tessa said crisply. 'I happen to think that men who feel the need to buy small, fast cars are just subscribing to the truth of toys for boys.'

'Toys for boys?' Curtis chuckled. 'I can assure you that I'm no boy! Haven't I already proved that by the kind of coffee I drink?'

'Yes, of course you have. Silly me. You're all man!' She slanted an ironic, sideways glance at him and just for a fraction of a second their eyes met and she felt a rush of unsteadiness. The glint in his eyes was wickedly, darkly teasing and for one heart-stopping moment it spiked into the very core of her, sending every pulse in her body shooting off into overdrive. 'You might want directions to my house,' she said in a very steady voice. 'I live out towards Swiss Cottage. If you—'

'I know where Swiss Cottage is.' He paused. 'Now to the original point of my conversation.'

Curiosity overcame apprehension at the oddly serious note in his voice and Tessa shifted to look at him. 'Yes. The favour you wanted to ask of me. What is it? If it's to do with working overtime, then I'm sure it won't be a problem, just so long as you let me know in advance what days you require of me.'

'Oh, well, some overtime might be needed but it's to do with my baby, actually.'

'Your *car*?' Wasn't this *baby* thing going a little too far? Boys with toys was bad enough but boys obsessed with toys was beyond the pale!

'No, of course not,' Curtis said impatiently. 'I'm talking about Anna!'

'Anna?'

'My mother *did* tell you about Anna, didn't she?'

Tessa thought back. She was certain she would have remembered the name. 'No,' she said slowly and thinking hard. 'Who is she?'

Curtis swore softly under his breath and pulled the car over to the side of the kerb, then he turned to face her. 'Anna is my daughter.'

'Your daughter?'

He swore again and shook his head, scowling. 'I take it my mother forgot to mention that little detail. Or rather chose not to.'

'But...I don't get any of this. *You have a daughter?* Are you *married*?' He didn't *act* like a married man. He didn't wear a wedding ring. And did married men have strings of sexy secretaries because they decorated their offices, with practical skills not of prime importance? Would his wife approve of that? Did she *even know*? Maybe, Tessa thought with a sickening jolt, they had one of those modern open marriages.

In the middle of her freewheeling thoughts, he interrupted with, 'A daughter, no wife. And I'm surprised this wasn't mentioned when my mother saw you.' The cunning fox, he thought indulgently. Had his mother thought that bringing up the question of his daughter and the spot of coverage that might be occasionally needed would have put off the perfect candidate? One of the reasons he had succumbed to her insistence on choosing his next secretary had been the little technicality that Anna was going to be on half-term for two weeks and his mother would be out of the country on a gadabout cruise with her circle of friends. Someone would be needed to help out with coverage should it become necessary and, in his mother's words, a flighty bit of fluff would not do.

'Anna is going to be home for a fortnight from her boarding-school tomorrow. Next week she's going to be coming into the office and I want you to take her under your wing. The following week should be fine. I intend to have the week off, but next week's a bit trickier with this trip to the Far East to source potential computer bases.'

'Boarding school.'

'Hence the fact that she has to come into the office. None of her friends live locally and my mother left the country a couple of days ago.'

Tessa couldn't take her eyes off his face. She could picture him as just about anything apart from a father. He had too much *personality* to be a father! Then she thought what a ridiculous idea that was.

'Are you following a word I'm saying?'

Tessa blinked. 'I just find it a bit difficult to comprehend...how old is...Anna?'

'Fourteen.'

'Fourteen. But you never talk about her...have pictures...' Was he *ashamed* of being a father? Was that why she was at boarding-school? Because she cramped his eligible-bachelor lifestyle?

'I have pictures in my wallet. Care to see them just to verify that I'm telling the truth and that she looks like a normal kid, no nasty side effects from my being her father?' He raised his eyebrows and Tessa blushed.

'No, of course not!'

'Can I ask you something?'

She nodded, still furiously examining the scenario that had unfolded in front of her.

'Did my mother know that you had raised a kid sister virtually on your own?'

'Completely on my own,' Tessa absent-mindedly amended. 'Yes. Why?'

'"A most suitable woman for the job."' He quoted his mother with a grin. 'Not only did you come with a sackful of references, but you were single, with a sensible head on sensible shoulders, and you had firsthand experience of communicating with a teenager. No wonder she failed to mention the little technicality of my daughter. You were so ideal for the job that she probably didn't want to jeopardise the chances of your accepting the offer.'

'I feel manipulated.'

'You'll have to mention that to my darling mother the next time you see her.' He pulled out slowly from the kerb, leaving her to her riotous thoughts for a while.

'But what exactly am I supposed to *do* with your daughter?' Tessa eventually ventured. If she had just one drop of his volatile blood in her, then she would be more than a handful cooped up in an office when she would rather be hanging out with teenagers. Tessa shuddered at the prospect lurking ahead of her.

'Supervise her. Give her little jobs to do. I'll be around for most of the week. When I'm not…'

'She can't possibly stay with me…!'

'Her old babysitter will take over. Don't worry. I have every faith in your abilities…'

CHAPTER THREE

ANNA was nothing like Tessa had expected. In her head, she had imagined her own sister at fourteen, but with Curtis's dark good looks. Gregarious, smilingly wilful and utterly boy crazy. Thrown into this mental picture was the added bonus of being the only child of a millionaire father. The equation was terrifying, not least because she knew from firsthand experience that she would spend the week tearing her hair out just to make sure that her beady eyes never ceased their constant supervision.

She had arrived on the Monday a full hour and a half before she should have just to make sure that she did as much of her own workload as possible. Just in case.

Curtis and Anna had finally come in some time about ten, Curtis flamboyantly explaining that he had made an essential detour to take his daughter out for breakfast, while in his shadow a tall, awkward teenager with her hair pulled back into a pony tail had hovered with her eyes lowered, staring down at her curiously old-fashioned shoes.

That had been three days ago. The boy-crazy handful of hormone-driven teenager had turned out to be a studiously polite and excruciatingly shy girl who seemed to enjoy working in the office more than she did leaving it and who only really smiled when her father was around. Then, she lit up like a Christmas tree.

'Anna?' Tessa looked at her now, head bent over the mighty stack of files that she had been allocated to go through, making sure that the paperwork corresponded to what was on the computer. 'Fancy you and I going out to lunch somewhere?'

Anna looked at her and smiled.

She had the prettiest face, Tessa thought, but the look was ruined by the hairdo and the clothes and the way she walked, slightly hunched as though ashamed of her height. Having gone through the wringer with Lucy, who had never believed in concealing her assets and who had been able to wield an eyeliner pencil at the age of fourteen like any professional make-up artist, Tessa knew that she should be vigorously counting her blessings that this one week was not turning out to be the nightmare she had expected.

However, it just didn't seem natural that Anna should be fourteen going on middle-aged.

'I've still got quite a few files to get done...' she said apologetically. 'I mean, I know it's only a pretend job but I'd still like to do it as well as I can.'

'It's not a pretend job!'

Anna gave her one of those shrewd, mature looks and Tessa laughed. 'It seriously is not! Those files are in a disastrous state! I don't think your father's last secretary was that bothered by something as mundane as filing.'

'No. I don't suppose she was.'

'Anyway, your dad's not back from the Far East until tomorrow.' Tessa stood up, switched off her computer and firmly began putting on her thick jacket. 'We can play truant for an hour or two.'

'Truant?' She giggled. 'Are you sure? I mean, won't you get into trouble?' The anxiousness was back. Teenagers shouldn't be anxious, Tessa thought with a pang, amused to catch herself wondering if she had been the same at that age. No, she hadn't. Her anxieties had come later. At fourteen, she hadn't been wild like Lucy, but she had been carefree and unburdened.

'Oh, I'll chance it. Now, come on. If we carry on debating this any longer, we'll talk ourselves out of it.' She waited as Anna stuck on her coat and quickly neatened her pony tail.

'How are you finding it?' Tessa asked as they settled themselves into the back seat of a black cab, heading towards the King's Road.

Anna shrugged. 'It's nice. I mean, I knew Grandma wasn't going to be around for the half-term and I'd be in the office with Dad, but I'm relieved that...' She chewed her lip sheepishly and hazarded a smile at Tessa.

'That what?'

'Well, I know what some of Dad's secretaries have been like. I mean, it's not that I've ever come in to the office to actually work or anything. This is the first time, actually. But sometimes I've come there to meet him for lunch or something, and well...'

'Gorgeous women in very short skirts can be a bit daunting,' Tessa agreed, astutely reading behind the hesitation. 'I know. I find that as well.'

'I could always see the way some of them looked at me, as if they couldn't really believe that I was his daughter or something.'

'You're beautiful, Anna,' Tessa said truthfully and Anna burst out laughing, a high, girlish tinkle that was all the prettier because it was so rarely heard.

'No, I'm not! My mum...now my mum was beautiful. I've seen pictures of her. She could have been a model, actually.'

Curtis's wife and Anna's mother had died when she was only a young girl in her early twenties. A freak skiing accident. This piece of information had been relayed to Tessa by Curtis, part of his explanation as to why his daughter would be working at the office for a fortnight in the absence of her grandmother. There had been no embroidering of details and he had shown no emotion, nothing whatsoever to indicate how the premature death of his young wife had hit him. Tessa had had no idea what the woman had looked like but she wasn't surprised to learn now that she had been beautiful.

'Dad likes beautiful women,' Anna was saying, her eyes glowing as they always did at the mention of her father. 'Grandma always says it's the Spanish blood in him. Actually, I don't believe that. I mean, there's no logical reason for it.'

The taxi had reached Sloane Square. Tessa had meant to have a nice, long lunch but now, on the spur of the moment, she decided that a little shopping wouldn't go astray.

'Shopping for what?' Anna asked curiously, barely glancing around her. 'Do you need anything?'

'I think I need an entire overhaul, actually,' Tessa told her, smiling. 'I mean, look at me! I need a new wardrobe!' She hadn't actually even considered this until now, but, thinking about it, she wondered whether it wasn't true. No one would guess that she was only twenty-eight. Lucy was forever teasing her about her old-fashioned clothes and Tessa had always laughed off the good-natured criticism, but now she wondered if she was as much of an anachronism as Anna was.

'I like the way you dress. It's…comfortable.'

'Hmm. Sounds exciting.' They began strolling up the road. It was a gorgeous day. Bright skies, cold and dry and almost windless. A perfect day for shopping.

With each step, Anna's interest in the shop windows grew, and when she finally pointed out something she actually liked Tessa instantly pulled her inside, away from the drab, well-tailored grey skirt towards a rail of reds and burgundies, brief, beautiful short skirts with tiny, boxy jackets to match. She overrode the protests, hearing the insecurity in Anna's voice as she shied away from trying to turn herself into something she wasn't.

A beautiful mother, a father who was singularly drawn to women because of the way they looked… It wasn't too difficult to see how a timid child could turn into an adolescent who was convinced of her own plainness. In her head, Anna had come to the conclusion that she couldn't possibly compete with her mother or with any of the women she had seen her father with, and so she had gone in the opposite direction. She had taken refuge in sensible clothes and sensible shoes and no trace of make up, ever, that might signal a willingness to enter into the dressing game.

Tessa could identify with all that so she couldn't quite understand why she just didn't accept it.

It was very gratifying, though, to see Anna stare at herself in the small burgundy suit, eyes wide at the change in her appearance.

'Maybe I'll give it a go…' she conceded, pulling out the cash that was hers to use.

By the time they finally made it to the restaurant, there was a clutch of bags. A three-hour lunch hour! They bolted down their food and returned to the office, literally like guilty truants, to find Curtis there, waiting for them.

Anna ran and flung herself at him, and Tessa stifled a heartfelt urge to groan.

'We're late,' she said quickly. 'I'm really sorry. My fault. I decided that I'd take Anna out to lunch and—'

'My fault, Dad!' She stood back and gestured to all the carrier bags that had been summarily relegated to the ground the minute she had laid eyes on the unexpected sight of her father. 'I've been shopping!'

She ducked down to the bags strewn on the ground and,

in the intervening pause, Tessa made her way to her desk and asked him crisply how the trip had gone, whether it had been successful.

The lifeless computer screen sent another jab of guilt at the extended length of time she had been out of the office. It was unheard of. She had never, but never, sidelined her duties in favour of something frivolous. The work ethic was so deeply ingrained in her that she very rarely even made personal calls from work, so skipping off on a three-hour jaunt was almost beyond the bounds of belief. Worse was the fact that she had been caught out.

'Very good.' Curtis was watching his daughter with amused indulgence, perched on the desk, arms folded.

He was wearing faded jeans and a long-sleeved cream jumper, the sleeves of which he had pushed up to the elbows. Tessa took it all in as she industriously switched on the computer and sat down.

His mouth was curved into a smile of loving expectation as he looked at his excited daughter. Improbable as it seemed, given his relentlessly single image, he was a doting father. He didn't often make it to any school things, Anna had told her, but, she had quickly excused, that was because he was always so busy at work. When he *did* visit her at school, he invariably arrived with armfuls of gifts, and of course he was always the centre of attention. Her friends swooned over him. She had related this with great pride in her voice, never implying that she had ever longed for anything else. Reading between the lines, just having Curtis as her dad gave her some kind of indefinable street cred amongst her classmates.

One by one, Anna pulled her purchases out of their bags. She was so pleased with herself that she barely noticed the shift in his expression.

Tessa noticed, though. The smile remained in place, but

his eyes were narrowed as he took in the little burgundy outfit, then the soft dark green skirt that Anna had said might come in handy for a school thing she had been invited to, then the series of vest-tops, perfectly respectable but certainly nothing like what she had possessed before.

Tessa was tempted to offer some reassuring explanation for the choice of clothes. They looked a lot smaller off than on.

'Well! What do you think?' The clothes had all been neatly laid out now. They presented a startling and colourful divergence from what Anna was currently wearing, namely a sober grey trouser suit and some flat black shoes.

Curtis was still trying hard to maintain his relaxed smile and Anna must have sensed it because her face shadowed and she asked in a smaller voice, 'Don't you like them?'

'How can he *help but* like them?' Tessa stood up firmly, drawing attention to herself and giving Curtis the most professionally warning smile she could muster. She walked across to where they were laid out and gave Anna's arm a little squeeze. 'You ought to have seen your daughter in these.' She folded her arms and, with her back to Anna, managed to consolidate the warning in her eyes. 'She looked fabulous. She's been so excited buying that the time just ran away with us.'

'They're lovely, darling,' he ventured, skirting round Tessa. 'But perhaps you'd better gather them up. No, better than that, after a hard afternoon shopping, why don't you get a cab back to my place? I'll be an hour here, tops, and we'll go out somewhere special for something to eat.'

'I'll wear one of my new outfits, shall I? Which do you think, Dad? Where will we be eating? Somewhere smart? I can wear the cream skirt and top with my coat. Just so long as we won't have to do too much walking.' She looked lovingly at the new shoes. The shoes had been the very last purchase and had benefited from being bought at the very peak of Anna's excited embarkment into the world of glamour shopping. They were fur-lined, pointed-tipped fawn boots that fitted lovingly to mid-calf and had instantly transformed her into fashion-model height.

'That's a very nice outfit, darling, but perhaps a little too skimpy for this time of year? And those shoes, well, they might get scuffed. You wouldn't want to ruin such lovely things on your first foray, would you?'

'I suppose not.' The voice was uncertain now. She slowly began to gather up the various bits, folding them neatly before returning them to their expensive bags.

'Perhaps we'll go somewhere casual after all.' He yawned expansively. 'Long-haul travel is hideously tiring.' He pushed himself away from the desk and gave Tessa a veiled look, oddly lacking in its usual warmth. 'And there's a stack of things to get through before I call it a day. Tomorrow we'll do dressy, shall we?' He beckoned Anna across to him and swamped her in a big bear hug. When she emerged, her face was once again beaming, all uncertainty gone like a scattering of rain on a summer day. 'Why don't you help Anna down with her parcels—' he turned to Tessa '—make sure she gets a taxi and then meet me in my office?'

Anna was full of it. Her father had returned early! She had spent the past two nights in the company of her ex-babysitter, now a married woman with a toddler of her own, and had expected to be spending another night in her company. Her eyes were shining at the prospect of an evening out with her dad. Tessa wondered whether she should gently steer her away from wearing any of the clothes that had certainly met with his disapproval, however much he had tried to mask it, and decided against it.

But she was curious. In every way, he was utterly and

disconcertingly laid-back. He did things his way, sweeping everyone else up into his own unique personality, yet there he was, frowning like a Victorian stereotype the minute his own daughter displayed the slightest inclination to be a normal adolescent.

And curiosity was not something she wanted to feel. Certainly not when it applied to her charismatic boss. Hopefully by the time she got back to the office he would have moved on to some other thought. He was like that, possessed of a restless, brilliant energy that sometimes leap-frogged with dizzying speed. Every so often, even when he was dictating something to her, she would see that look in his eyes and realise that his mind was working ahead of itself, had jumped ahead to something new.

No such luck.

That clever, questing mind had focused on his daughter's brand new wardrobe and was staying there. The look on his face said it all as she walked into his office and shut the door behind her.

'So you and my daughter have been getting along.'

She could have faced up to him a little more confidently if he had chosen to sit at his desk like any normal human being. However, Curtis being Curtis, he was stretched out on the sofa, eyes closed, hands lightly linked behind his head. Tessa had to swivel the chair round to face him and then found herself reluctantly compelled to look at him, at that ridiculously good-looking face and those even more ridiculously long eyelashes.

'She's a lovely young woman. You must be very proud of her.'

'She's fourteen.' He opened his eyes and slanted her a glance. 'Not yet a *young woman*.'

'And what would you call it?'

'I would call it *a kid*.'

Tessa didn't answer.

'I asked you to provide Anna with some simple office duties to occupy her days. I didn't ask you to take her on an elaborate shopping spree.'

'You're right. You didn't. I'm sorry. She's been doing so well and I thought it might be nice for us to go out to lunch somewhere and before I knew it, we were shopping.'

'Before you knew it...'

He was looking at her now, his eyes narrowed slits. Ranting and raving, Tessa could manage. This soft, menacing voice, however, was a lot scarier.

'You're a secretary. Not a mother substitute for my daughter.'

Tessa drew in a long, deep breath and sat up straighter. 'I had no idea that part of my secretarial duties included babysitting the boss's daughter,' she said quietly, 'but that's fine. She's hard-working and enjoyable to have around. But having strayed from my original job description, I think it's a little unfair to start drawing boundaries. I don't know why you're so upset because Anna bought one or two things to wear. Teenagers *like* shopping, in case you hadn't noticed.'

'Of course I *know that!*'

'Then what's the problem? If it's the amount of time I took off, then I'm more than happy to make up for it by working late tonight and tomorrow night.'

'It's nothing to do with the amount of time you had off,' he said irritably, swinging himself up from the sofa and glowering at her on his way to his desk. He stood there, as if debating whether to sit down or not. 'And you're being deliberately obtuse. Since when have you ever seen me crack a whip because someone's running a bit late? More work takes place in these offices than in any other place I know, and that's *without* me having to pull the heavy-handed card.'

Tessa had now swung her chair around to face him. He still hadn't sat down. Maybe, she thought, he felt that if he sat down at his desk he would be more inclined to get down to the business of work. He propped himself up on the desk, palms flat on the gleaming surface, and continued to frown darkly.

'Then what is it?'

'I don't like the clothes you encouraged my daughter to buy.'

Tessa didn't know whether to shout at him or burst out laughing. Where had this puritanical streak come from? Here was the man who had thrown away the book of rules, who encouraged every aspect of creativity in the people who worked for him, who *had a sofa in his office,* for goodness' sake, *just in case he wanted to sleep*, just in case *he decided to spend a night in the office*. He must, she supposed, *somewhere,* keep a store of conventional suits, but she had yet to glimpse one.

Why on earth would he object to his daughter buying a few trendy clothes? There was nothing offensive in a single one of the outfits Anna had chosen. In fact, Tessa had dryly compared her choices to the ones Lucy had been making at the same age and marvelled at how she had managed to deal with her lovable headache of a sister all those years ago.

So where, she wondered, was the problem?

'I would never have expected it of you,' he said accusingly, and her head shot up at that.

'Meaning...?'

'Meaning that I thought I could trust you not to lead Anna astray!' He pushed himself away from the desk and began prowling around the room while Tessa sat completely still in her chair, counting to ten and refusing to swivel her chair in every direction just to keep up with his restless progress.

'Aren't you overreacting just a bit?'

The silence that greeted this was deafening. Tessa felt the hairs on the back of her neck stand on end and she realised, too late, that not having him within her line of vision was a major disadvantage.

She was oblivious to his stealthy approach until she felt the chair swivel round and found herself facing him, inches away from him, in fact, as he leant over her, caging her into her chair, leaning into her. She pressed herself into the back of the chair but, with nowhere to go, he remained close enough for her to feel his breath fanning her face.

Cool-headed composure shot through the window at a rate of knots, and in its place came a surge of panicky agitation. She wanted to push him back, but just the thought of her hand making contact with his hard chest made her quail.

'Maybe overreacting's a bit strong…' she retreated weakly. 'You're her father…'

'Damn right I am!' Curtis growled. 'I'm her father and there's no way I'm going to see my baby dressed like a tart!'

Tessa's eyes opened wide at this blatant display of double standards.

'A tart?' she spluttered. 'Did you actually *look* at the stuff Anna bought?'

'Sure I looked at it!'

'Those happened to be very expensive designer clothes!' Which was hardly an overstatement. At the time, Tessa had baulked at the price tags merrily dangling from the clothes, but she had swallowed back the temptation to hurry her charge along in the direction of more affordable places. This was a world she had never seen before. A world in which a fourteen-year-old girl had all the money she wanted at her disposal and was innocently ignorant of any need to go cheaper.

'I don't care if they were hand-finished by the Great Man up There himself!' he bellowed. 'I don't want my daughter wearing any of it! She was perfectly happy in clothes that *covered her up!*'

'How do you know that?' A delicate matter. Anna had confided in her that her father had always seen her as his little girl. He brought her back lavish gifts of coats and jackets that were beautifully tailored and cost the earth, but were not exactly the height of fashion, and she had never thought to rebel because she adored him.

'Because *she's never complained!*' He strode away from her and settled himself behind his desk.

Tessa released a long sigh of relief. Her legs were going stiff from sitting in the chair, rigid with tension, but a well-honed sense of survival told her that any mention of actually getting down to the business of work would be a big mistake. Curtis was still chewing on his thoughts and her options were basically reduced to staying put and trying to dodge the verbal missiles or else feigning a sudden, extreme illness.

'Well?' he prompted. 'What have you got to say to *that*? Hmm?'

'You're right.'

He looked at her suspiciously. 'Are you trying to calm me down?'

'No!' Tessa lied, protesting.

'Because if you are, I can tell you from now that that's one sure-fire way to get me enraged.'

At least he was no longer breathing fire and brimstone, though. Having the full force of his anger directed at her had been scary. Had that been yet another one of those elements of his interesting personality that his mother had casually mentioned? An ability to make other people aware of just how high their adrenaline levels could go? Working for a firm of accountants was beginning to seem like a stroll in the park!

'Look,' she ventured tentatively, 'Don't you think you're a little guilty of double standards?'

'I have no idea what you're talking about,' Curtis informed her with sweeping arrogance.

'You go out with beautiful women who wear provocative clothes. You employ beautiful women whom you *expect* to wear provocative clothes! Well, with the exception of me, obviously. You *like* attractive, glamorous women. I just don't see anything wrong with your daughter making the most of her youth. She's way too sensible to want to dress like a tart but she's *not a kid,* whatever you want to think! She can't go straight from frilly petticoats into slacks and jumpers a middle-aged woman would wear!'

'Said your piece?'

'I most certainly *have not*!' Lord, but how this man had the talent to get under her skin! 'How can you be so...*so authoritarian* when it comes to your daughter and *so relaxed* with everyone else?'

'Because she's my daughter. Believe me, I've seen first-hand how boys grow up looking at girls dressed in next to nothing...'

'Oh. Right.'

Black brows met in an irritable frown at her capitulation. But she didn't quite know what to say. They could keep going round in circles for hours because the plain truth was that Curtis wanted to protect his daughter and his version of protection was to insulate her behind a severely grown up image that would guarantee that no boys would be pounding at her door. While Anna was not unhappy with it, Tessa wondered whether she might be in time, whether her rebellion would take place later on and be all the more disastrous for that.

'Let me show you something.' He opened the bottom drawer of his desk, rummaged around, keeping his eyes firmly glued to her face, and eventually pulled out a photograph, which he slapped down on the desk in front of her. 'Have a look. Go on. It won't bite.'

Tessa tentatively went to look at the picture. A woman gazed back at her, her face propped thoughtfully in one hand, her mouth forming a little smile. She looked in her early twenties and was spectacularly beautiful. Silver-blonde hair framed a face that was perfectly chiselled, the sort of face that made men stare and then stare again and made women sigh with discontent at what they had been dealt. Laughter lurked just behind the pensive expression, as if she was holding back a boundless love of life.

'Chloe.' Curtis reached out for the photograph, glanced once more at it and stuck it back into the drawer.

All Tessa could think was that there was something poignant about him keeping that picture there, close at hand. Was that why he was so drawn to beauty? Because he had never really moved on from his wife?

'I was a kid when I met her and she was overwhelming, dazzling.' He grinned fondly at the memory and Tessa saw, for one second, a huge void open up in front of her, the void of being sensible and never dazzling anyone, then she was back to normal, listening, watching his expressive, gorgeous face as he spoke. 'We leapt into love as though tomorrow might never come, but of course it wasn't love. More like lust. We had a supremely lusty relationship. By the time she became pregnant, we were already drifting apart. Her looks, you see, that flamboyant way of hers…she couldn't resist the heads that were continually turned in her direction, she couldn't resist that pull she had over other people, something that made her want to just keep going. Anna grounded her for a while, but in the end it wasn't enough. I watch Anna pulling those clothes out of those bags and I see how easy it would be for her to start thinking that maybe education isn't that important, maybe having fun and all the attention that comes with being beautiful is a hell of a lot more appealing.'

'You're seeing things in black and white,' Tessa said uncomfortably. 'She'd hate to think she had disappointed you with her new wardrobe.' She stared down at her slender fingers, at the neatly trimmed fingernails shiny with clear polish. 'I won't take her shopping again and I wouldn't have if I had thought for a minute that you would have such violent objections to her splashing out on some pretty routine teenage gear. Not even really teenage, as a matter of fact. Just different from what she's accustomed to wearing.'

Why did he get the feeling that he was being verbally outmanoeuvred? Curtis looked at the smooth, bland face and frowned. He opened his mouth to say something, thought better of it and grunted instead.

'We'll have to agree to differ.'

'We will,' Tessa agreed, lowering her eyes, 'and, of course, there'll be no more corrupting shopping sprees.'

There was perfect acquiescence in that response except, he thought, for his perfect secretary to be acquiescent, she should also have been chastened, and chastened she certainly was not. In fact, in her own quiet way, he got the sneaking suspicion that she was reprimanding him. He moved swiftly away from the whole contentious subject and for the next hour they worked solidly and swiftly. As she was standing to leave he leaned back in his chair and asked her what she thought of his plans to consolidate a base in the Far East.

'Have you been reading up on this?' he asked, when she had finished her impressive monologue and Tessa relaxed enough to smile at him.

'Of course I haven't ''been reading up on it''. I've always preferred a good work of fiction to a computer magazine. No, I just happen to have a brain in my head and an ability to voice an opinion.'

'Which is why you're turning out to be such a good little secretary,' Curtis replied smugly. 'I'm going to have to admit to my mother that she may just have got it right when it came to hiring you. I never thought I'd hear myself say this, but a guy can get tired of beautiful girls sticking the wrong files in the cabinets and typing at a snail's pace.'

'I didn't think the misfiling and slow typing was a problem,' Tessa came back quickly, bristling under the composed surface. 'I thought Lizzie and Marge just picked up the slack.'

'There's way too much gossip in this office,' he said, grinning. 'I'll have to have a word.' He was an unrepentant sinner, though. Tessa, however, was in no mood to indulge him. From what she had seen, he was far too indulged already. He had been indulged at birth, by being blessed with staggering good looks, and from that it had probably only been a matter of time before self-assurance and charm had stepped into the equation. Add a brilliant mind and the world, she reckoned, had probably been his oyster from when he was a toddler.

'Will that be all?'

'You've gone prune-mouthed on me again.'

'Prune-mouthed?' Tessa flushed.

'You know what I mean. Tight-lipped. Like a schoolteacher inspecting a particularly offensive pupil.'

Tessa knew exactly what he meant and that in his own forthright way he had no compunctions whatsoever in airing his views, the way he always did. In all fairness, she knew that she could give him a piece of her mind and he wouldn't bat an eyelash, but naturally she wouldn't. She wouldn't fly off the handle and she certainly would never dream of telling him that being compared to a tight-lipped schoolmarm really hurt. It was just a little too near the mark for comfort.

She wasn't about to let him totally off the hook, however. She drew in a deep breath and said calmly, 'If you don't like my demeanour, then perhaps you'd like me to go?'

'Now you're offended.' He swept out of the chair and was standing by her before she had time to beat a tactical retreat. His voice was gushingly solicitous. 'And I like your demeanour!' He placed his hands on her shoulders and Tessa felt a peculiar surge of heat race through her, sending her heart into furious overdrive. 'It's very…bracing.'

Bracing? Was that a step up or a step down from tight-lipped? The worst of it was that he genuinely didn't recognise why she would be offended. Because she wasn't an airhead, she was virtually sexless. Infuriatingly, it bothered her.

'That's a huge improvement,' Tessa said, forcing a smile.

'Good. And I want you to know that you're a valuable member of the team.'

'Thank you.' She wished he would just remove his hands from her shoulders. Horrifyingly, he tilted her face to his and gave her a crooked smile, a smile that could turn lead to jelly.

'You're welcome. I like the way you speak your mind, I like your opinions and I don't want you to go away thinking that I ever make unfavourable comparisons between you and my previous secretaries. I use the term secretaries loosely.'

Something funny was happening to her inside, something confusing and frightening. 'Okay.' Quick agreement, quick exit.

He released her and she nearly fell backwards. 'Brilliant!' He remained where he was, watching as she left his office, only calling out behind her, 'Just don't see that as a licence to go shopping with my daughter, though!'

This time Tessa closed the door just a little too loudly behind her.

CHAPTER FOUR

A QUIET weekend at home would be just what the doctor ordered.

Curtis's outspoken comments, not meant to be insulting but insulting anyway, had got to Tessa and she didn't quite understand why. In fact, she spent most of Saturday trying to work it out. It was proving annoying, as if the question were like a demon sprite, willing to be boxed in for intermittent periods, but only so that it could leap out at her just when she wasn't expecting it.

Lucy had gone away for the weekend and the house was blissfully calm.

At five-thirty, Tessa returned to the house after a hectic but essential visit to the supermarket. When she had been at her last job, she had always done her shopping on a Thursday night after work. Her hours had been fairly regular there and she had slipped into a routine that had suited her.

Now...

She had to do several trips from her small, second-hand car to the kitchen and it was half an hour before she had finally unpacked the last of the groceries, then she sat down wearily on a kitchen chair, tipping her head over the back and closing her eyes.

The demon sprite lunged out at her again.

She found herself thinking about him, thinking about the intense beauty of his face, the way his eyes crinkled when he laughed, the way they narrowed when he was thinking about something. She found that she had even committed to memory his various little habits, like the way he always yanked open the bottom drawer of his desk whenever he wanted to lean back in his chair and stretch out his long legs.

Tessa shook her head impatiently, snacked on a bar of chocolate, even though she knew that she would be eating in a couple of hours' time and was in the shower, in the process of washing her hair, when she heard the sharp buzz of the doorbell.

Lucy, was her first thought as she reluctantly turned off the shower, stepped out and wrapped herself in a bath sheet. Had she come home early from her weekend away? Lucy had a problem with keys. She continually went out and forgot to take them with her. Whenever she was faced with Tessa's wrath at having to drag herself out of bed at some ungodly hour to let her in, she invariably smiled sheepishly and swore never to repeat the same mistake again.

Her hair clung damply around her face, which was in a definite scowl as she pulled open the front door, lips parted to inform her sister that this was *absolutely the last time* she was going to go through this predictable charade.

No words came out. Something did but it was akin to a choking, strangled noise.

On the doorstep was Curtis, dressed in an impeccable charcoal-grey suit with a very conventional white shirt peeping out from between the lapels of his jacket. On one side was a highly disgruntled-looking daughter and on the other a leggy blonde with hair tumbling in disarray past her shoulders and a full complement of war paint. Her glossy red lips matched her glossy red fingernails, which in turn matched the glimpse of glossy tight dress that was only loosely covered by a startling terracotta-coloured silk trench coat. On anyone else the combination of colours would have brought on a sudden rush of nausea in the casual observer, but on her the clash of colour was dramatic and overwhelming.

Tessa shrank back and mortified colour crept slowly up her face. She still couldn't seem to string two words together to form a sentence.

She stared dumbly at Curtis and for once he didn't give her that lazy, amused grin.

'Do you normally answer the door with nothing but a towel wrapped round you?' he asked, levering his eyes upwards to her face.

'I thought it was my sister.' At last, she had managed to corner some vocal cords. 'What are you doing here?'

'You'd better let us in before you catch a death of a cold,' he said reasonably. Tessa was very tempted to slam the door on their faces, but he had already wedged one foot on the doorstep. She stood back, burning with embarrassment.

'Excuse me. I need to change.'

'Oh, don't put yourself out for us,' Curtis said, grinning now and raking his eyes over her semi-clad body in one wicked sweep. Just the sort of look she could imagine him giving the blonde at his side. That thought was enough to put frost into her voice.

'The sitting room's through there. I'll just be a minute.' She tried not to be affected by the thought of three pairs of eyes following her progress up the stairs towards the bedroom, but she was trembling when she shut the door behind her and hurriedly grabbed some clothes from the wardrobe. A pair of faded jeans and a long-sleeved black tee shirt that had faded through numerous washes.

Her hair was still a wet mess but, rather than waste time blow-drying it, she did what she sometimes did on a weekend to get it out of the way. She braided it into two plaits that just about reached her shoulders.

Now she looked about sixteen, but frankly she didn't care. How dared he waltz into her house without calling her beforehand to find out whether he was welcome?

Because he was shrewd enough to guess the response, a little voice said.

She slipped on some bedroom slippers, some garish black and gold pointy-tipped things that looked as though they would have been better suited to life in a Middle Eastern harem, which had been one of her birthday presents from her sister four months previously.

The three unwanted visitors were in the sitting room, although, when Tessa walked in, it was apparent that only one of them was at ease. Curtis had made himself at home in one of the comfy chairs while the other two were perched in rigid discomfort at opposite ends of the sofa.

'Sorry to barge in on you like this,' he said pleasantly.

'You didn't have to.' Tessa sat down, uneasy in her own house, which was ridiculous. 'You could have telephoned first.' She turned to Anna, caught her eye and smiled. 'How are you, Anna? Recovering from your first week at work?'

Anna made a valiant attempt to smile back but her eyes slid across to her father and the corners of her mouth turned down. It was a pout full of sulkiness. And, Tessa noted, she was back to wearing her neat, background clothes. A long-sleeved shift dress in brown, dark tights and flat brown shoes with a distinctive and recognisable thin gold designer band at the top.

'I would have if I had had the opportunity, but coming here only became an option on the drive over. Didn't it, Anna?'

'I just don't want to go to the theatre this evening,' Anna

said stiffly, 'and I don't know why you're making such a big deal of it.'

Tessa wondered what this minor domestic tiff had to do with her, but she refrained from saying anything. Out of the corner of her eye, the vision in red vibrated in silence on the sofa, her body language screaming discomfort.

Curtis must have read her mind because he finally introduced the woman, Susie, his date. His attention was obviously not on her, though, because he immediately reverted to his daughter, frowning as he looked at her. 'Anna insisted on the way over that we come here,' Curtis said patiently. She couldn't have imagined him ever getting cross with his daughter, with whom he was effusively affectionate, but he was cross now. 'She threw a tantrum, in fact.'

'I did not throw a tantrum, Dad! You just won't listen to me!' Tears thickened her voice and Tessa wanted to groan in dismay. 'You *said* that the two of us would be going out!'

So that was it. Poor Susie, the innocent participant in this small family drama. The girl looked close to tears herself and, having resolved to get rid of her guests as quickly as possible, Tessa now heard herself asking whether they wanted anything to drink. She could only offer wine in terms of alcohol.

'I'll come with you!' Anna sprang to her feet and disappeared out of the sitting room before her father could protest, and protest he most certainly was about to, judging from the expression on his face.

'I'm tired of it!' was the first thing Anna said as soon as Tessa was in the kitchen. She plonked herself down on a chair and glumly propped her chin in her hand. 'He promised we'd go out for a night, just the two of us, and then, lo and behold, the next thing I hear is the doorbell and there's Barbie-doll Susie on the doorstep!'

Tessa rested three wineglasses on the counter and turned round to face Anna. She, uncharitably, thought that the description was very accurate. In her head she had idly wondered what sort of women Curtis was attracted to. In the flesh, she realised that she hadn't been very far from the predictable truth. Glossy packaging without much of an intellect inside. She wondered whether his daily life was so full of creativity and challenge that beautiful bimbos were restful, a panacea at the end of a long working day.

She reminded herself sternly that, one way or another, speculation like that went nowhere because his private life was no concern of hers.

'He must have just forgotten about the theatre tickets, Anna,' she said gently, 'and I'm sure he didn't think you'd react the way you have. Surely you've been...well, out with him in the company of one of his girlfriends?'

'Of course I have.' She sighed laboriously. 'But when I was younger, I never minded, and anyway, he never made a habit of it. I know I'm behaving like a kid, but...'

'You *are* just a kid.'

'A teenager! And that's another thing.' She stuck her chin out belligerently, daring Tessa to side with her father. 'He said that the clothes we bought together don't suit me, that I look better in less gaudy stuff, but yet he has the *nerve* to go out with women who dress like...like teenagers!' The unfairness of it caused the threat of tears to become reality, and, try as she might, Tessa could find no easy comforting words to that adolescent protest because she basically agreed with his daughter.

She sighed inwardly and marvelled at how a man as clever and as worldly-wise as Curtis Diaz could be so hideously inept when it came to reading his own daughter and understanding what made her tick.

'You know what fathers are like,' Tessa said, playing down the situation. 'They can be a bit overprotective.'

'Was yours? I mean, when you were my age?'

'Different philosophy,' she hedged, thinking of her parents, who had quite rightly suspected that too many stringent guidelines ended up gestating bigger problems than allowing their girls a little leeway here and there, just enough never to make them feel as though they were being imprisoned against their will.

'I hate arguing with Dad.' Anna looked at her with such misery that Tessa's heart constricted. 'I don't see all that much of him. I mean, I'm at boarding-school and he does his best to see me whenever I'm on holiday or half-term, but, really, it's not an everyday thing. I just want us to go back to being how we were, but he can be such a tyrant!'

'Not always.' She poured wine into the glasses and offered Anna a glass of something light, which she refused, as she did the offer to come back into the sitting room, preferring to remain in the kitchen.

'We've ruined your evening, haven't we?' she asked in a small voice and Tessa laughed.

'I'd only planned on some pasta on a tray in front of the television. The most relaxing thing I can do when Lucy's not around.' She fished a circular tray out of a cupboard and carried the wine into the sitting room where active conversation was under way between Curtis and his Barbie doll, as Tessa now found herself thinking of the other woman.

'I'm dropping Susie back to her place,' Curtis announced, standing up and ignoring the wine. 'There's no point even thinking of going to any theatre now. The play will already have started anyway. Is there a chance you can hang on to Anna for about forty minutes?'

Tessa did not want to get caught up in this. She didn't want his private life to begin infiltrating into hers and she didn't want to find herself reluctant referee in a disagreement between him and his daughter. On the other hand, what choice did she have? She remembered Anna's forlorn face and felt sorry for her, so she just nodded.

Susie had her hand resting on his, and her face, raised to his, was disappointed. She looked, in fact, as though she had just been put through a wringer, as though, suddenly, from being the woman who was all dressed up, she had become the woman who was all dressed up with nowhere to go. And on top of that she couldn't even command her date's attention, which was very firmly focused on a sullen fourteen-year-old tucked away in the kitchen.

Curtis was back almost to the minute but the trip had done his tension no good. He was still unusually brooding when he stepped into the hall, glancing towards the small kitchen at the back.

'Thanks for that. Where is she? I'll take her home and let you enjoy the remainder of your evening in peace.'

'Bed.'

'Bed? You were going to enjoy your Saturday evening in bed?' Hard on the heels of that came a crazy thought, *And who's the lucky man?* He wasn't looking down at his efficient secretary who always had her hair pinned back and always, but always, wore neat little suits and blouses carefully buttoned all the way up. He was looking at someone with calm eyes but a stubborn chin, someone with glossy hair and a figure that managed to be boyish but very, very feminine.

He felt a dangerous stirring in his loins. Never had he felt this sudden, uncomfortable prickling under his skin when in the company of a woman. For a man who was highly complex underneath the easy charm and self-assurance, Curtis had never been drawn to his female counterpart. He liked his women to be easy on the eye and easy on the intellect.

He turned away abruptly and was aware of her following him into the sitting room. 'Anna? So where is she?' he demanded sharply, which drew an instant bristling response from Tessa.

'She's upstairs in my bed. Asleep.'

'At this hour?'

'She was upset, Curtis. I told her to head upstairs to wash her face and when she didn't come down I went to check her to find her fast asleep. Like a baby.' They stared at one another and Tessa felt her heart begin to race. He had disposed of his jacket, but he was still disturbingly tall and dark, especially in the confines of her house. She had a sudden feeling of being invaded and she had another spurt of resentment that he had brought his private life here, in her house, where she was defenceless.

'I'll go and wake her up.'

Good idea, Tessa thought to herself, and then you can both head off to wherever you had planned on going. Anywhere but here would suit her fine.

'Maybe you should let her sleep off her stress for a little while,' she said reluctantly. 'You can always come back if you want to take your girlfriend out. I'm home all evening and I don't mind keeping an eye on her.'

'You're home on a Saturday night?' For some reason that gave him quite a satisfied feeling and he relaxed enough to grin at her.

'Yes, that's right. Home on a Saturday night. How dull of me.'

'I never said that staying in was dull. In fact, I rather enjoy staying in sometimes myself...'

The implication behind that hovered tantalisingly in the air between them, the implication that stay in he might but he would be doing it in the company of a woman, a Susie clone. Champagne in bed. Certainly not pasta on a tray in front of the television.

'You never answered my question,' Tessa repeated coldly. 'I can babysit Anna if you'd like to pick up what you were doing with your girlfriend.' Neither of them had sat down. Curtis had strolled over to the window and was perched on the ledge, arms folded over his muscled chest. Tessa had stopped in mid-stride in the middle of the room and hadn't moved.

'Oh, I think Susie's better off where she is. No point making her endure my company tonight.'

'I doubt she would consider it hard work,' Tessa muttered sourly and he tilted his head politely to one side in a parody of someone doing their best to catch what was being said.

'I can't hear you when you mutter like that.'

Tessa panicked. What was she supposed to do with him if he stayed in her house till his daughter woke up? She had had enough experience of fraught teenagers to know that they could retreat for a quick nap only to fall into a deep four-hour sleep. Lucy had had a talent for just that when she had been younger. Tessa thought of Curtis Diaz prowling through her house for four hours while she tried to make conversation, and every ounce of self-composure went into immediate meltdown.

'I said that I thought she looked...well, very let down... that your plans for the evening had changed... I'm sure she'd appreciate you going over and, honestly, there's no point you being here if Anna's sleeping...' She wondered whether he had detected any desperation in her voice. He was still gazing at her with every semblance of attentiveness, though she had a feeling that she was getting precisely nowhere. 'And I…I hadn't planned on any company. There's nothing to eat in the house…'

'Nothing to eat in the house?'

'Well, nothing fancy…' He had managed to make her plausible-enough excuse sound ridiculous, as though a rooting-through of her cupboards and fridge would unearth nothing more than a few crusts of bread and some mouldy cheese.

'I'd prefer to stay here. I understand your evening's been spoiled, but I'm relieved you had nothing planned…'

Tessa felt her cheeks burn at what she thought was amusement in his voice. 'Lucy's away for the weekend…I enjoy the peace and quiet…'

'So you said. Now, what were you planning on eating?'

'Nothing! I mean, *nothing much…*'

'Nothing much. Sounds fine. Unless you'd rather I went and brought us back something? There's a supermarket I noticed on the high street. I'm pretty sure it'll still be open.'

'No, that won't be necessary,' Tessa said in a strangled voice. Visions of him returning in his fast car with shopping bags for an evening in cooking together was enough to bring her out in clammy perspiration.

It occurred to her that she had never entertained a man at home, not in the sense of make a meal together, sit and watch television. She had had a scattering of dates but no one important and she had always been happy to either go out somewhere or meet in a crowd. No wonder this man found her so amusing, accustomed as he was to the women he went out with.

'I was just going to make myself some pasta,' Tessa said

reluctantly. 'If you wait here, I can stretch it to two. I guess.'

He could hardly blame her for the lack of graciousness in her offer. He had descended on her with Anna in tow, ruined the peaceful evening she had planned, and she had now been further inconvenienced because his daughter had decided to fall asleep in her bed, leaving him here like a spare part.

That being said, Curtis didn't for a minute contemplate taking her up on her suggestion that he return to his date for the rest of the evening.

'I'll go and check on Anna,' he informed her, 'and pasta sounds great.'

'You can watch a little television if you like. Nothing much on and I'm afraid we don't have cable, but…quiz shows can be quite entertaining…provided you don't want to think too much…' She knew that she was gabbling on, but his eyes were mesmerising, that was the only word to describe it. She had to inhale deeply and turn away to break the connection, then she hurried top speed towards the kitchen, hearing him as he headed up the stairs towards the bedroom.

Calm down, she told herself! She took a few steadying breaths and switched on the portable CD player on the kitchen counter. Lucy found it hilarious that her big sister actually listened to *easy listening* music, but right now it was exactly what her jangled nerves needed.

A soft, soothing melody filled the little kitchen and she began to slow down, humming quietly to herself as she began chopping onions and mushrooms and tossing them into the plastic bowl next to her.

She imagined Curtis sitting in the room watching a tedious quiz show and couldn't stop herself from smirking.

In all her life, she could think of no one less suited to

being condemned to enforced immobility in front of a boring television programme. Curtis Diaz had way too much energy surging through him for that. Well, she couldn't help but think that there was a spot of justice to be found in the fact that he had wrecked her evening, intruded upon her private life despite her having made it absolutely clear from the word go that it was off limits, only to now find himself forced to sit down and kiss his own thrilling evening goodbye in front of the box. She began peeling the cloves of garlic, sniggering heartily at the thought.

The grin was still on her face when she swung around to grab a frying-pan from the cupboard, only to hear the subject of her musings say, in his smoky, sexy voice, 'Care to share the joke?'

Tessa looked up in sudden shock. She had been so absorbed in her pleasant thoughts, so lulled by the melodic strains of music, that she had had no inkling of his presence. She hadn't heard him approach! How long had he been there? Watching her? It made her feel as though he had been standing, spying on the workings of her mind.

'I thought you said that you were going to go and watch some television!' she accused hotly, snatching the frying-pan from the cupboard and proceeding to give him her most withering look.

'No, actually *you* said that I was going to watch television, so that I could be tucked safely out of the way...' He grinned with wicked amusement as his barb homed in with staggering accuracy.

Tessa recovered her aplomb quickly. 'And why aren't you?'

'I did make an effort...' He shrugged and walked into the kitchen where, infuriatingly, he began poking around in the bowl of chopped vegetables while Tessa watched in affronted silence. 'But...' he spun around and looked at her '...absolutely nothing on...'

'Not even a quiz show?' she asked sweetly.

'Oh, yes, a couple of those. I wasn't convinced. Can I help?'

'Yes. You can go and watch TV and leave me in peace to get this food ready.'

'I like your taste in music. What is this? Compilation?' Without asking, he gathered up the stack of CDs that she kept on the counter by Lucy's assortment of herbal tablets, and made himself at home on one of the kitchen chairs so that he could sift through them and give her his valued opinion on each and every CD.

'I think we should stick this one on,' he announced, waving one of the CDs at her in a satisfied manner. 'Lots of old numbers. In fact, I'm a little surprised you're not into more modern music!'

Tessa made an inarticulate noise and began her work with the frying-pan, some butter and garlic, and the vegetables.

With staggering arrogance, he put on the CD he wanted to hear, a compilation of old soul songs, from way back to Otis Redding, and the next thing she felt was his warm breath fanning her neck as he asked her for a dance.

Already hot from standing in front of the stove and having to contend with his presence in the kitchen, virtually right under her feet, Tessa now felt a surge of blazing warmth invade her body in a rush.

'Don't be ridiculous!' she snapped, jabbing the vegetables in the frying-pan with overdone savagery.

'What...not now? Not with me? Or not ever with anyone...?'

'Shut up!' She daredn't lift her eyes to his, even when she was aware of him drawing back. If he even glanced at her flushed face, she knew that he would read every shred of wild confusion inside her, every treacherous tug of excitement filling her veins like poison. 'Why?' he asked interestedly. 'Am I touching on a raw nerve? Don't tell me that you've never danced to a beautiful piece of music in the privacy of your own four walls? With a man?'

Actually, no.

Tessa added some herbs and cream to the mixture and stuck a saucepan of water on to boil for the pasta, hiding behind the pretence of busyness to avoid answering his prying questions.

'You're not *a man*,' she said, turning around to face him, arms folded protectively across her breasts. It was very important that she get that straight right now, she decided, before her wayward mind started taking too many unwelcome detours. Yes, he was attractive. Well, formidable, really. Yes, she had been aware of his sex appeal before now, but not like this, not in the claustrophobic confines of her own house. She had a deep-rooted fear that if she didn't lay down her boundaries, something from him, some oozing magnetism, might just seep into the walls around her, into the furniture and lie waiting in ambush for her whenever she returned home.

'You're not a *man*,' she repeated, 'You're *my boss*. You're the person I happen to work for, who just happens to have found himself in my house for reasons beyond my control, and it's no good you giving me a little speech about how you like to know your employees inside out, about how you like them being three-dimensional. I don't feel any need to be three-dimensional with you. So, no, I won't dance with you and whether I ever have at home with anyone is none of your business!'

That had wiped the grin off his face, she noticed. In fact, it seemed to have temporarily deprived him of the power of speech, which should have been good, should have been a clear pointer that she had won this particular battle, but for some reason the look on his face now was even more unsettling.

He had gone absolutely still and there was a dangerous quality to his stillness that had every pulse in her body racing.

'Wh-which isn't to say that I *resent* your probing…' she stammered, lying through her teeth. 'I mean, I know that it's part and parcel of your personality…'

'Being nosy?'

'Curious,' Tessa amended hurriedly. 'Interested in everyone and everything…which brings me to my cooking…you'll be interested to know that I'm not awfully good at it…' She fervently prayed that he would take the bait, accept the olive branch she was holding out, which was by way of apologising for her criticism while sticking to her guns. He did. He gave her one of those heart-stoppingly crooked smiles and suggested wine with the meal, reminding her that none of them had touched what she had brought in earlier, before he had driven Susie home.

Curtis could almost hear her shudder with relief. He was pretty relieved himself. Since he had arrived at the house, he had been too aware of her for his own good. Too aware of her clean smell, the enchanting freshness of her looks, the enticing depths of her personality which fought him off and beckoned him at the same time, and just for a minute there, when she had firmly put him in his place, reminded him that he was nothing more than her boss and a highly inconvenient one at that, he had felt as if someone had punched him in the stomach. Yes, he *was* her boss. A little technicality he didn't intend to forget. Despite his predilection for sexy secretaries, he had never been tempted to sleep with any of them. Why he felt compelled to hire them in the first place was something he had never questioned, although he was inclined to agree with his mother that it was all to do with delegation of duties. He could get away with giving them the minimum to do, ensuring that company confidentiality was never threatened. It had always suited him. Tessa was already winning his trust, slowly but surely, when it came to work. Jeopardising that on an insane whim would be madness. Added to which he was not, by nature, attracted to women like her, women of discreet charms, however alluring those charms might seem on the odd occasion. Like right now.

He struggled to recover his usual easy charm and not let his attention stray from her flustered face to the gentle swell of her breasts and the slimness of her legs encased in their tight jeans.

'Some wine, then. Food smells good, whatever you say…' He disappeared towards the sitting room, to rescue the untouched wine she had poured earlier on and returned with the tray. 'Gone a bit tepid, unfortunately…'

'No problem. There's some ice in the freezer.'

That unsettling moment had passed as ice was fetched and the table set and the food brought out, occupying most of the table top even though it was just one dish of pasta, one of salad and some dressing.

Or had it?

They sat opposite one another, but Tessa could feel her cheeks aching from having to force herself to smile. Just a few centimetres too far, and their knees would touch. A major disadvantage with a tiny kitchen table, she decided. To avert that possibility, she tilted her legs to one side, but every fibre in her being was aware of him, aware of the flex of his muscles as he dug into his food, aware of the way he twirled the spaghetti on his fork, aware of his dark eyes resting on her face during mouthfuls.

They talked about music, pleasant, unthreatening chit-chat that made her think about dancing with him. They talked a bit about work, about his ideas for the Far East, which made her wonder how he would look after a few weeks in the hot sun. Even darker and sexier than he did now. From that they moved easily into chatting about holidays abroad, and after she'd drunk two glasses of wine in record time she heard herself elaborating on her childhood, on how things had changed after her parents had died, on places she had seen and all the ones she wanted to but probably never would. At the back of her mind she knew that she would regret all the confidentiality in the morning, especially after her robust speech about keeping the lines between them clear.

But she didn't want any pregnant pauses to creep into the conversation between them.

'I hope it hasn't been too much of a strain,' Curtis said, when they had finished eating.

'What hasn't?'

'My being here with you tonight, taking advantage of your hospitality and good nature...'

He knew that she would blush. He also knew that he should be listening to his head, which was telling him to leave as soon as possible, even if that meant waking his daughter up.

'I...no, of course not...it's been fine...'

'Good.' He stood up and waved her down when she was about to follow suit. 'Don't even think about it! You cooked and I'll wash. Fair's fair!' He raked his long fingers through his hair and looked at her steadily. It required a superhuman feat of concentration. Her mouth looked so damned tempting, half parted like that...

'Why don't you go and check on my daughter?' he said

thickly, turning away. 'I'm a quick washer. By the time you get back I'll be done.'

Tessa stood up, thankful for something to do that required her to be out of the kitchen. 'Just make sure you do a good job,' she said lightly, addressing his broad back and wondering how she could possibly know that he was smiling. 'I don't accept shoddy work.'

She had expected a nightmare evening. It hadn't been. It had been good, and she wasn't sure whether that was worse…

CHAPTER FIVE

TEN minutes later Tessa returned to the kitchen to find that the washing-up was certainly being done but in a cavalier fashion that entailed stacks of dishes balanced precariously on the draining-board. She watched, enjoying the sensation of being the observer rather than the observed, as Curtis's hand hovered, trying to locate a safe spot on which a wine-glass could be deposited without bringing the whole fragile balancing act crashing to the floor.

'Anna's up,' she announced. Without intervention, she doubted that the glass would survive in one piece. Before he could add it to the worrying pyramid of dishes, she grabbed a tea-cloth and removed it from his hand.

'Oh, good,' Curtis said, taking time out to watch her as she quickly dried the object and then moved on to remove crucially placed items back to the safety of the kitchen counter.

'Up and very apologetic about just falling asleep like that. Apparently she's been up very late most nights, doing emails to her friends, and what with exhaustion from work and all the stress of this evening, she just closed her eyes for one second and nodded off. I told her that she could have a bath and freshen up before she came down.'

'Well, let's hope she's in a slightly better frame of mind when she emerges,' Curtis replied, rinsing the last of the cutlery and dumping it into the upturned frying-pan, which was the closest thing to hand.

'I think she's hoping pretty much the same about you, actually.' Tessa carried on with the drying-up, not looking at him. 'There's a method to washing dishes, in case no one's ever told you,' she said, breaking the silence with nervous chatter. 'It usually involves using those convenient slots in the plastic for plates and the little attached rectangle at the front for cutlery.'

'I say that when it comes to washing dishes, speed is of the essence. I have no reason why Anna thinks I might be in a bad mood.'

'Because you were in one before she decided to lock off and go to sleep?' Tessa prompted, sticking the last of the dried-up dishes into cupboards and moving to stand behind one of the chairs.

'It's not every day a man gets attacked by his daughter because he happens to want to bring a woman along with him on a date.'

Tessa gave him a long, dry look and he returned it with one of innocent bewilderment.

'I really don't think she was objecting to you wanting to bring *a woman* along with you,' Tessa informed him succinctly. 'I think it was the *type* of woman you wanted to bring along.'

'Oh, I see.' He looked upwards, calculating how long Anna would be having a bath. Not long, from the sound of footsteps just above him. 'Look,' he said urgently, 'I really need to have a chat with you about this whole sorry situation. You seem to have built up some kind of rapport with my daughter and—'

'Forget it.' Yes, he was her boss, and, yes, there were limits. She could get a whiff of where he was heading with this one and she didn't like what she smelled. It had the fishy odour of trying to entice her into influencing a fourteen-year-old girl.

'Forget *what*? You haven't even let me finish!'

'I think I hear your daughter descending,' Tessa said

with heartfelt relief as the footsteps heralded a rush into the kitchen, where Anna immediately skidded to a halt.

'Sorry, Dad!' It was an apology without being apologetic and she eyed him warily, trying to gauge his mood from a safe distance. But her feathers were still ruffled. Not ruffled with the normal adolescent truculence and hostility. After a lifetime of absolute adherence to her father's wishes and adoration from afar, truculence and hostility would not be within her range of emotion. But Tessa could see all the signs of teenage rebellion, nevertheless.

'If you'd said you were tired, I would never have suggested we go out,' Curtis responded, shoving his hands in his pockets.

'It wasn't about whether I was tired or not.'

Tessa sighed.

In an hour's time they would both have forgotten their argument, but in an hour's time she would still be dealing with the fallout of having been dragged into involvement.

'Perhaps it's time both of you...sorted out your differences at home? By which I mean your own home?'

Two pairs of eyes swivelled towards her, neither displaying any wild enthusiasm for her suggestion for them to leave.

Tessa groaned inwardly.

'It's getting late,' she tried again, 'and Anna must be starving. She hasn't eaten, after all.' She turned to Curtis, appealing to his paternal side.

'I really don't want to go to a restaurant in this...' Anna said, flicking her head and staying her ground.

Tessa was puzzled. 'In what?'

'This.' One hand indicated her outfit in a smooth sweep.

'Oh, right.'

'You look beautiful, Anna. I told you that earlier!'

'Dad, you've been telling me that since I was a baby!'

'You've been beautiful since you were a baby!'

This was going nowhere fast. Having survived dinner, Tessa now recognised it seemed as though imminent departure was becoming tangled up in a quagmire of two people who, probably for the first time ever, had hit a rough patch. And they had hit it in her house.

'Would you like me to fix you something to eat, Anna?' she interrupted their exchange of words reluctantly.

'Have you got any pizza?' Anna asked hopefully and Tessa shook her head. 'Well, could you perhaps send out for some?'

'There's a pizza place just a few minutes' drive away,' Tessa said, brightening up. 'Why don't the two of you…? Well, it's not as though it's anything fancy…you needn't worry about your outfit there…'

'It's Saturday night. It's a pizzeria.'

'Right.' Tessa nodded in comprehension. She remembered the syndrome well. When *she* was fourteen and still enjoying her youth, she too would never have ventured into a casual, adolescent-ridden setting in anything but her most screamingly casual clothes. And when *Lucy* was fourteen and heading anywhere where she might possibly be seen by other teenagers, her outfits had involved whatever jeans had happened to be in fashion, the least practical of her tops and shoes that most normal people would have found it difficult to walk in.

'Explain, please,' Curtis interrupted from the sidelines of what looked like a female conspiracy, and Tessa turned to him.

'Pizzerias on a Saturday are usually home to teenagers wearing less…well, formal clothes. Anna thinks she might stand out a bit…'

'Stand out!' Curtis exploded incredulously. 'Stand out?

Yes, sure you'll stand out but only because you're a cut above the rest!'

Anna greeted this by turning on her heel and stomping out of the kitchen, leaving her father with a look of stunned amazement on his face. This quickly changed to glowering accusation as he looked at Tessa.

'This is all your fault,' he informed her. 'We never had these ridiculous problems until you decided to take her on a shopping trip. She was always fine with the clothes she had.'

'I think you need to go and talk to her,' Tessa returned with as much calm as she could muster given the unfairness of his accusation.

With a curt nod, he disappeared only to return minutes later. 'Where's your phone book?' he asked, pulling his mobile phone out of his pocket. 'It seems that eating out *anywhere* tonight isn't an option with my daughter. She's decided that she wants to sit in front of your television and eat some pizza so I've told her that I'll order some in.'

'Sit in front of *my* television? Why can't you both go home and she can sit in front of *your* television and eat the pizza?'

This was getting ridiculous. From a quiet night in, enjoying the peace of having the house to herself, she now found herself entertaining two people at loggerheads with one another, one of whom evoked all the wrong reactions in her. Worse, she could cope with him when he was at work, could cope with him when he was teasing her even though it made her insides squirm. Could even cope with him, just, when he was flirting with those dark eyes and that sexy smile. Flirting came naturally to him and meant nothing. In that context, it was possible to distance herself from some of the devastating effects of the odd wayward smile, the occasional crinkling of his eyes when he looked at her.

However, coping with him when he was like this, baffled and seemingly at a loss as to how to deal with a situation, was proving a nightmare. She wanted to plunge right in and stroke all his troubles away. Just the thought of that made her gulp with a hysterical swelling of pure alarm.

This was the essence of the charmer, she reminded herself. And the man was charm personified. It was a quality that couldn't be pulled out of a hat and then shoved back in; it was something that was there, always, enticing and beckoning. It was the quality that made women want to be near him, made them want to continue contact long after any relationship might have gone pear-shaped.

'Phone book?' he reminded her, bringing her thoughts to a skidding halt.

'I'm really very tired.' One last stab, she thought, one last attempt to propel him and Anna out of the door, leaving her in peace.

Curtis looked at his watch and then looked at her. 'It's not even nine-thirty as yet.'

'Yes, well, not everyone keeps late nights.' A deafening silence greeted this and it didn't take a rocket scientist to work out what was going through his head. Either he had reached the right conclusion, namely that she didn't want him around, in which case his active mind would already be jumping ahead to reasons and maybe, just maybe, coming up with the right one. Or else, she would be confirming his sweeping assumptions that she was as dreary as he thought she was, someone who retired to bed before ten with a cup of cocoa when all the world was out having a good time on a Saturday night.

Tessa fetched the phone book from the little bookshelf behind her and handed it to him.

'What did you say the name of that pizzeria was…?'

She gave it to him and watched in despairing silence as he rapidly phoned and placed his order before clicking off his mobile and sticking it back into his pocket.

'Forty minutes,' he informed her. 'I guess the place is so busy with hordes of appropriately dressed teenagers that the food orders are moving a little slowly.'

Tessa hesitated, torn between ignoring the light-hearted remark, made at her expense, and diving into a serious debate on his short-sightedness in not listening to what his daughter was trying to tell him. In the intervening silence, he solved the dilemma for her.

'Not funny? I suppose you think I'm making fun of a serious situation?'

'What I think doesn't matter and what you do doesn't concern me.'

'Very lofty sentiments,' Curtis mused, eyes narrowing on her. 'Must be easy getting through life when you can detach yourself from annoying situations with such ease.'

'I'm not detaching myself from anything,' she responded hotly. 'I'm just telling you that you have to sort out these temporary problems with Anna yourself. I can't be of any help.'

'You were a great deal of help when it came to rampaging the shops with her in hot pursuit of skimpy clothes.'

Tessa nearly laughed. Did he really see what those women he entertained wore? Had he really noticed Susie's outfit, which just about managed to cover her? If he thought Anna's new wardrobe was comprised of skimpy clothes, then how would he describe his girlfriends' choice of garments?

Silly assumption, she thought. What was good enough for his girlfriends was certainly not good enough for his daughter. Beneath the sharp, unconventional exterior, there beat the heart of a pure traditionalist.

'Would you like a cup of coffee?' Tessa asked, resigning herself to yet more emotional involvement in his life. 'Tea?'

'Coffee would be good.' He shoved himself away from the counter and sat at the kitchen table, watching in silence as she made them both a mug of coffee.

It was as clear as daylight that she wanted to get rid of them, or rather of him, he suspected. The decent thing would have been to leave her in peace, to enjoy the uneventful evening she had planned, but he decided that he really did want to talk to her about Anna, whose behaviour was as mysterious as it was unexpected. He also realised that he was rather enjoying himself here, watching her pad around preparing a meal, listening to her voice her opinions with absolutely no regard for whether she trod on his toes or not.

It was refreshing, he decided.

Refreshing to be in the company of a woman without the inevitability of sex.

He looked at her lazily from under his lashes, noting the slenderness of her body, the perfect jut of her rear, which was always so cunningly camouflaged at work underneath those asexual suits she insisted on wearing. There was nothing obvious about her, he thought. She didn't announce her sexuality, but look just a little deeper and there it was, as subtle but as fragrant as a summer breeze.

'Hello?' Tessa couldn't resist tossing his sarcastic mantra back at him. 'Is anybody there?'

'Hilarious,' Curtis responded, his mouth twitching at the corners. 'Sit down. You're making me nervous hovering over me like that.'

Tessa laughed, not one of those cultivated tinkling

laughs, but a proper laugh. 'I don't think it's possible for anyone to make you nervous.'

'Because, as I've mentioned before, I'm one hundred per cent man?'

'Because you're self-assured and arrogant.'

Curtis eyed her narrowly, trying to work out whether she was joking or being serious and realising that he didn't like it in the least that she thought he was arrogant. Coming from another woman, it wouldn't have bothered him in the slightest, but coming from her…

'Self-assured, yes. Arrogant, no.'

'Well, you seem to make a pretty good job of assuming you know exactly what's right for Anna without even considering that you might just be wrong.' Tessa sat down, rested her elbows on the table and sipped some of the coffee.

She hadn't been making an observation on *him*, he realised. She had been making an observation on one aspect of his behaviour. He shifted irritably in his chair, reluctant to engage in practical conversation, wanting to prod deeper into her and the workings of her mind. Insofar as they related to him.

'Why would I be wrong? I know my daughter.'

'You shouldn't have told her anything about the clothes she'd bought. I assume you did?'

'I mentioned that they seemed a little unsuitable.'

'Well, far be it from me to offer an opinion on how you bring your own child up…'

'But…?'

Tessa shrugged to lessen the impression that she might be voicing unwanted views. Also that his affairs might impact on her much harder than she wanted them to. 'But you should let her wear what she wants to wear, within reason, and please believe me when I tell you that Anna wouldn't push the boat out. She barely glanced at any of the ridiculously hipster trousers kids these days wear or any of the super-tight Lycra tops that leave nothing to the imagination.'

Curtis, head tilted to one side, half heard the gist of her remark. He just heard the telling way she referred to *kids*, as if she were a woman in her fifties instead of someone in their twenties.

'"Kids these days?"' he teased softly, holding her startled look and enjoying the sudden stillness hanging in the air between them. 'You're not exactly an old lady, Tessa.'

'No. I know that. I know I'm...' *A highly qualified and competent secretary, fully computer literate and with the references to show for it.*

'Yes...?' He cocked his head to one side.

'I'm pretty responsible for my age,' she conceded. The doorbell rang. In the nick of time, she felt, because she had uneasily been aware of ground shifting under her feet. She sprang to her feet, only to see that he had similarly stood up and was fishing into his trouser pocket for his wallet.

'You stay here,' he commanded. 'I'll pay for the pizza.'

Stay in the kitchen? Waiting for him to return so that he could resume their conversation, which was slowly sending her into a state of frantic panic? No way.

As soon as he had exited she went to the cupboard and quickly prepared a tray with plate, cutlery, a stack of paper napkins and a glass of orange squash. They coincided in the sitting room, where Anna was engrossed in an inane program featuring two muscle-bound women who seemed to be competing with one another in a series of frankly ridiculous tasks. She made a few appreciative noises when the pizza was put in front of her, barely aware of the pair of them looming to one side.

Curtis opened his mouth to ask what level of nonsense

she was watching, thought better of it and signalled to Tessa that they leave.

When she stood her ground, he tugged her gently but firmly out of the sitting room, keeping his hand on her arm until they were back in the kitchen.

'I get the feeling we might cramp her style if we stay in there with her,' he said, pushing the kitchen door behind him and killing the last vestige of noise wafting in from the television.

'Which is something you would never dream of doing.'

'Touché.' He was still holding onto her, enjoying it, and as though she had suddenly realised that she shrugged him off and sat back down.

'Okay. I get your point.' He reluctantly sat back down. 'Maybe I'm a bit overprotective and now's the time to start cutting the apron strings a bit.'

'That might be a good idea,' Tessa agreed, relieved that the conversation seemed to be back on an even keel. Discussing Anna was bad enough when it came to blurring the boundaries between Curtis and herself, but drifting into the unknown territory of discussing each other was off the scale altogether.

'I mean, lay down too many laws and you can sometimes find that a teenager will attempt to break them all.'

'Is that what you had to cope with when it came to your sister? You must have been pretty green round the gills when you found yourself having to deal with a teenager.'

'I coped,' Tessa informed him briefly.

'Ah, but I'm intrigued. How did you? Cope, I mean?' He smiled encouragingly. The urge to find out more about this woman was becoming irrational. His mind, which frequently drifted off in the direction of work whenever he was in the company of a woman, seemed to have developed extraordinary focusing ability.

His eyes wandered to her mouth, to the slender column of her neck. In his head he began to remove her top, bit by very slow bit.

'Lucy was a headache, but essentially a pretty good kid. No drugs, no alcohol, or at least not much, no staying out all night. I loosened some of her boundaries and she respected that. I think she knew that we'd both been thrown into a new situation and we had to help each other along the best we could if we were to survive. I gave her freedom within limits and she gave me her obedience within limits.'

The little speech fizzled out into the silence, which stretched unbroken until she became aware of the low hum of the fridge, just vague background noise suitable for magnifying the stillness.

'I suppose we've just…just got ourselves into a pattern…' she tripped on, losing the thread of what she was saying with each murmured word. 'She's the frivolous one and I…I indulge her…'

'And who indulges you?'

Tessa was aware of colour invading her face, a hot, burning flush that seemed to originate from within the deepest part of her. She had rested both her hands on the table and was now aware of exactly how small the table was. Certainly not big enough for the two of them when he was staring at her like that and she was responding in classic overwhelmed female tradition.

Then he did something so shockingly intimate that the breath literally caught in her throat, almost as if her brain had shut down and could no longer give the message to her lungs that she should inhale.

He reached out and gently, oh, so gently, began stroking the side of her thumb with his finger.

For such a small gesture, it was unbearably erotic. She felt the dampness of arousal spread through her and when she finally did manage to breathe, it was laboured and painful.

'Who does? Are you going to tell me?' he coaxed softly, and she had to blink several times before she remembered what he had been saying in the first place.

'I…I don't need indulging…' Her own whisper reached her ears with all the force of her forbidden excitement. For the life of her she couldn't remove her hand even though her head was telling her to scramble her wits together and run away.

'I don't believe that…' Curtis murmured. 'Not for a minute.' His finger moved from her thumb to the sensitive flesh of her wrist.

'No boyfriend?'

Fascinated by the movement of his finger, Tessa shook her head slowly.

'Ever?'

She shrugged. 'I've had boyfriends, but nothing serious…' Her lowered eyes flickered and he felt a sharp burst of exultation and an arousal that was so hard that it was almost painful.

Without removing his hand, he slid out of his chair until he was squatting right in front of her, looking up at her. And still he continued that lazy caress of her arm, just a feathering of sensation that was sending her body into a vortex of sensuous excitement.

'Poor baby,' he murmured huskily.

Tessa half opened her mouth to find a reply to this throaty observation, but before any words could emerge he straightened and she gasped as his mouth hit hers with a blinding, urgent passion that stifled every rational thought.

The force of his kiss pushed her head against the chair and she wrapped her arms around his neck, drawing him closer to her and returning the kiss with all the pent-up craving that had been stalking her for weeks.

He pushed her hair back so that he could nibble her ear and his warm breath had her squirming on the chair, panting softly with her eyes closed, arching her neck in open invitation for him to do what he was doing now, trailing his tongue against it, feathering it with kisses while his hand smoothed her taut skin above the waistband of her jeans.

Jeans that felt too tight, too clinging.

It was bliss when he parted her thighs with one hand so that he could position himself between them. Then he circled her waist with his hands, running them up along her ribcage and finding the restriction of her bra as impeding as she did.

Lord, Tessa thought on a soundless groan, this is madness. But as he pushed up her shirt and pushed up her stretchy bra, madness and her ability to deal with it were lost in a swirl of intense, aching desire.

She had never felt like this before. Had never even come close.

In a daze of wonder, she half opened her eyes as his mouth found one nipple and he began to suck it. Her body slid rapturously down a couple of inches in the chair and she surrendered to the ecstasy of his warm, wet mouth exploring the tight buds of her breasts, loving them with exquisite tenderness.

She was experiencing a sensation of total meltdown, and it was only the sudden noise of the television that alerted her numb senses to the awful reality of what they were doing and to the even more awful reality of Anna leaving the sitting room.

With a squeak of horror, Tessa pushed him away, yanked down her top and her bra in one swift movement, over breasts that were still throbbing, and scooted to the furthest corner of the kitchen.

God, she couldn't look at him. She just couldn't. It would be like looking her worst nightmare in the face and knowing that it wasn't about to go away.

How could she?

No point blaming him. She had responded enthusiastically, *desperately,* and the thought of that was like a flood of icy water rushing over her, straight through her body and right into her veins.

When she finally did raise her eyes Anna was pushing open the kitchen door and Curtis was back in his chair, outwardly as collected as she was torn apart inside.

'It's finished,' Anna said, yawning. She had brought through the remaining pizza in its box on the tray and she deposited it on the kitchen counter, resoundingly unaware of any atmosphere in the kitchen.

Tessa was deeply and profoundly grateful for the inherent selfishness of most adolescents, who rarely noticed anything that didn't pertain to them.

'Really?' Tessa's mouth ached as she forced herself to smile and appear relaxed. 'Who won?'

'The gigantic one with the straight black hair.' Another yawn. 'She had the muscles of a body-builder.'

'You're tired,' Tessa said lightly, arms folded, holding herself in and still not daring to look across at Curtis, who was sitting forward with his elbows resting on his thighs. 'So am I. In fact, I'm really going to have to be very rude and insist you both go home so that I can get some sleep.'

'Dad?'

'Uh. Yes.' He glanced at his daughter, then seemed to give himself a mental shake before he stood up and stretched, an unconsciously graceful movement that Tessa resentfully thought summed him up. The way he looked, the way he spoke, the way he moved, it was all a work of Art and she had succumbed with shameful alacrity.

'I'll be out in a minute, Anna. I just want to have a quick word with Tessa about some work stuff she needs to do for me on Monday.'

There was nothing Tessa could do to prevent Anna from leaving the kitchen and, since she would have to face him, this seemed as good a time as any. At least the experience wouldn't last longer than a few minutes, not with his daughter waiting outside and twiddling her thumbs.

'That should never have happened,' was the first thing Curtis said when the kitchen door had closed behind Anna. He stood up and crossed the small distance separating them while Tessa steeled her features into a mask of frozen impassiveness. 'And I'm sorry.'

He raked his fingers in angry frustration through his hair. He had wanted and he had just gone right ahead and taken, he thought, sickened by himself. He hadn't stopped to think that this woman was different, that this woman made him feel as though that whole-relationship-thing, as he cynically referred to it, might just be possible. If he could have turned the clock back, he would have, but he couldn't.

And now she was freezing him out. He gently placed his finger under her chin and, with a sharp flick of her head, Tessa backed away and looked at him coldly.

Hadn't he called her *poor baby*? Before he had touched her? Poor little Tessa, all alone on a Saturday night, with nowhere to go. Had he thought that seducing her might have been an act of kindness? He wouldn't even have had to go down the complete road, just a kiss and a grope, enough to inject a little colour into her drab life and a little amusement into his. The pain of humiliation raced through her, making her giddy.

She would hate him, she thought, but only after she had

hated herself. For closing her eyes and sipping from the poisoned chalice. It was no good telling herself that her body had let her down, that her emotions had been too awesomely powerful for her to withstand.

'I think we should both forget what just happened.' She was surprised at how composed she sounded. 'Things got a little out of control, that's all.'

'That's all?'

What more did he want her to say? she wondered savagely. Did he want her to confess how much he had blown her over? Did he want her to massage his already mightily healthy ego by agreeing that she had very nearly become yet another notch on his much-indented bedpost?

'That's right. I may not be as old as you or as experienced...' she shuddered at the dreadfully personal confidence she had shared with him in her heady moment of passion '...but nor am I a silly little fool.' She dismissed the unfortunate incident in a casual shrug. At least, she desperately hoped that she gave that impression. 'These things happen.' Except not to her. To him, yes. To those women with their short, short skirts and come-to-bed eyes, yes. But she knew herself well and the unfortunate incident went far beyond just being unfortunate. It was something that had opened her eyes to the very real fear that she was falling for her boss. Her wildly exciting, unorthodox and utterly unsuitable boss.

'These things sometimes happen, but—'

Tessa saw the yawning, hideous chasm open up in front of her and rushed in to cut him off in mid-correct assumption.

'Never again.' She drew herself up to her full height and mutinously stuck her chin forward. 'It was a mistake and I have to have your word that it will never happen again or else I shall have no option but to leave your company immediately.'

'Fighting talk,' Curtis murmured. 'What makes you think that I would be the perpetrator of any further mistakes?'

It took a few seconds for the meaning of what he had said to sink in, and then she uttered a little dismayed grunt. He was nothing if not direct. He was reminding her that she hadn't exactly been an innocent angel, passively having to endure his advances. She thought of her enthusiastic responses and a tidal wave of pure shame washed over her.

'Because I never make the same mistake twice,' she said forcefully. She had never even been in a situation like this before but even so she knew that she couldn't afford to let her emotions overtake her sanity as she had just done.

'I'll be taking next week off,' Curtis said, moving towards the kitchen door and opening it. 'Having some quality time with Anna as I haven't seen as much of her this week as I wanted to.'

Tessa breathed a sigh of profound relief. She managed to unglue her feet and follow him out of the kitchen, and even managed a smile when they were standing at the front door.

'It's been brilliant working for you,' Anna enthused, making it difficult for Tessa not to be moved by the sincerity. 'Guess I'll see you next time I'm home? Which would be Christmas?'

'I hope so,' Tessa said, directing her attention to Anna but reserving the significance of her words for Curtis.

'I'm sure Tessa will have no reason to leave the company before then,' Curtis murmured to his daughter, conversing with Tessa just below the surface, as she had done with him.

Because, Tessa thought, closing the door on them and then leaning heavily against it to stop herself from subsiding to the floor, he certainly would give her no reason to go. Those twenty ruinous minutes would be history for him because they had meant nothing, hence he could assure her, truthfully, that they would not be repeated.

For her, however…

She let her legs do what they wanted to do and sat down, back to the front door.

Thank goodness he wouldn't be around for a week. She could put everything in perspective and, really, she was not a silly, emotional girl. It was a calming thought. She simply wouldn't allow Curtis Diaz to get under her skin and the fact that he had played her for a fool was mortifying…but helpful.

After all, who, in the end, could be attracted to a man who had had no qualms in making a pass at a woman out of pity?

CHAPTER SIX

'YOU'RE not still here!' Curtis stopped in the middle of the office and frowned. He, himself, wouldn't be here but for the fact that he had forgotten his mother's Christmas present in his desk drawer.

Tessa looked up guiltily and flushed.

Yes, here she was. Still. At four-thirty in the afternoon when the office was deserted because everyone had either gone home already or else had joined the group who had chosen to have a last lunch and drink at the pub down the road before the company closed for the Christmas break.

'I was just about to leave,' she said, switching off her computer and shoving things into her drawers, tidying up her desk. 'I wanted to finish all my work before the break.'

'How industrious,' Curtis said dryly, strolling over to where she was doing her best to ignore him by concentrating hard on flicking through the remnants of her filing tray. 'I think what's left can wait, don't you?' He reached out and circled her wrist with his fingers, stopping her in mid-tidy.

Tessa's heart did that familiar, lurching thing and she could feel every nerve in her body tense as she stilled and looked at him, at the lazy, perceptive eyes boring into her.

The past seven weeks had been a trial by ordeal. Her ordeal. After that incident in the kitchen, he had stuck rigidly to her request that they forget about what had happened. She had not seen him for the week after, when he had been out of the office, taking his daughter on various excursions, although they had spoken on the telephone regularly, at least twice a day, purely on work matters. When he had come back, things had returned to normal, the only difference between them that she could see was that he was slightly more aloof than he had been.

They settled back into a familiar routine, although he no longer pried into her private life. She was left to assume that the ease with which he had forgotten what had taken place told its own telling story about how much the misplaced episode had affected him. Not much.

'Why didn't you come to the pub with us?' he was asking her now. 'Don't tell me you preferred to stay here and make sure all your pencils were neatly arranged in your drawer before you left? I thought your excuse was that you had to go and do some last-minute Christmas shopping?'

He had released her hand and Tessa made good the opportunity to skirt round her desk and head towards the coat stand in the corner of the room. She could feel his eyes following her every movement.

'I do have a bit of shopping to do, actually,' she flung lightly over her shoulder as she put on her coat.

'Oh, yes. What?'

'This and that.' She shrugged and then, wondering whether he was going to stay on, hovered for a while. 'Are you going to be working now?'

'Yes,' Curtis informed her gravely. 'I thought I might just get in a couple of hours' work. You know, tidy my desk and get all my pens and pencils in some kind of order for when I return after the Christmas break.'

Tessa lowered her eyes, but her mouth was twitching. However much she knew that she should keep her distance from him, there were times, as now, when he made her want to grin. And it had been for ever since he had adopted that teasing tone with her, the one that made her toes curl and the hair on the nape of her neck stand on end.

'That's very important,' she returned with equal gravity. 'There's nothing worse than getting back to your desk after a little break to find that all your stationery's in a muddle.'

'Actually, I just came to get my mother's Christmas present from the drawer. Hang on a minute and I'll come down with you.' He disappeared into his office, fetched a box without bothering to turn the light on, and reappeared, still in his coat, which he hadn't removed.

Tessa picked the first neutral subject she could think of as they walked towards the lift, and asked him what he had bought for his mother.

'An antique brooch and some matching earrings,' he said. 'For some reason she's into things like that.' He was tossing the box lightly from one hand to the other. Tessa caught it in mid-air and handed it to him.

'I don't think you should be doing that,' she said sternly. 'What if it drops and breaks?'

'The shop has very carefully wrapped the contents in tissue paper,' Curtis said, pocketing the box, 'so I don't think there's much chance of that happening.' He looked at her sideways, amused and irritated to see the way she huddled against the side of the lift as though to stand any closer to him might bring her into contact with an infectious disease.

'What last-minute things have you got to buy?' he asked, stepping aside when the lift shuddered to a stop so that she could brush past him. In a minute she would be gone, eaten up by the black wintry evening outside. 'What are your plans for Christmas?'

'A stocking filler for my sister and not much, to answer your questions.' Tessa turned to him and forced herself to smile. What was *he* going to be doing for Christmas? He wouldn't be seeing Susie. She knew that for a fact. He and Susie were no longer an item. The company grapevine, with its usual irreverent efficiency, had long ago gleaned that Curtis and his Barbie doll had run their course. For the past four weeks, bets had been on as to what the replacement would look like and Curtis, fully aware of the furious speculation, had responded by informing them that he would be trying out celibacy for the foreseeable future. This in itself was sufficient to raise the tempo of the guessing games.

'Not much…hmm…sounds a little dull…'

Tessa had an instant replay in her head of him kissing her in the kitchen, caressing her, pushing up her shirt and bra so that he could attend to her breasts. All because he had felt sorry for her because she was dull. A spurt of anger made her turn to him.

'And what are *you* going to be doing?' she enquired with barbed sarcasm. 'Have you got a thrilling few days lined up? I mean, you never said…Susie the Barbie doll is no longer around, so who's the replacement? Have you decided to go for a different model this time or stick to what you know? Someone blonde and busty with a vocabulary that just boils down to the one word *yes*?'

She could have kicked herself when he smiled a long, slow smile at her.

She turned away abruptly and headed towards the exit, aware that he was following her, his footsteps as stealthy as a cat's.

'I didn't realise you'd been following the progress of my love life with as much gusto as everyone else,' Curtis murmured alongside her as they stepped out into the freezing embrace of a winter in full throttle. 'I don't recall ever seeing you adding any contributions to the board in the corridor.'

The board in the corridor had been the bright idea of one of the computer whizkids. It charted each and every speculation from anyone who cared to have input and entries ranged from petite brunette with Hollywood aspirations to older woman with a yen for toy boys. Curtis eyed it with amusement every time he walked past and occasionally wrote his own cryptic message on it himself.

'That's because I haven't,' Tessa said tartly. 'I'm about to head to the underground, so have a good Christmas.'

He fell into step with her. 'Now I'm hurt,' he said sorrowfully. 'I thought you cared...'

The mildly flirtatious teasing had been conspicuous by its absence and now it made her already heated skin begin to prickle with all the dangerous awareness she had successfully slapped down over the past few weeks.

'Well, you were wrong. Why are you following me?'

'Because I'm trying to persuade you to come and have a drink with me considering you never managed to make it to our little lunchtime party earlier.'

'I'm sorry. I can't.'

'Because you need to get that important stocking filler.'

'That's right.' The underground was now within sight, visible between the hordes of people who were also apparently on the search for last-minute Christmas gifts. The sight of that many people made her feel a little ill but now that she had told him she needed to shop, she had little choice but to honour the white lie, with him walking next to her like an unwanted shadow.

'In which case, I think I need to get a few things myself. We could go and have that drink afterwards.'

'No, we cannot!' Tessa refused vehemently, stopping to glare at him and irritating the flow of people who were forced to break their hurried stride around them.

'Scared, Tessa?' he taunted softly. 'You didn't manage to make it to the company do a couple of weeks ago either. A sudden cold, if I remember correctly?'

'I have to go, Curtis.' She spun around, blinded by rage

at what she could only assume was mockery in his voice. Never mind how clever and good looking and incisive and witty he was, she thought furiously, he was still the Man with the Oversized Ego.

She hurtled away from him, struggling against the sea of people, caught up in them as they began to cross the road as one on the go ahead of the little green man from the traffic lights.

Her thoughts were spinning off on a tangent, paying scant attention to the pavement, when her leg buckled under her. The crowd that had virtually carried her along in its surge from one pavement to the middle island had failed to be so accommodating as they'd hurried towards the far pavement.

Tessa gave a groan of pain, tried to maintain an upright position, but, with no one to hold on to, she slid inelegantly onto cold, hard tarmac and, had it not been for a couple of steel arms lifting her out of her embarrassed misery, she was convinced that people would simply have stepped over her in their haste to finish the rest of their Christmas shopping.

The owner of the steel arms spoke in an all-too-familiar voice and Tessa groaned again, this time with heartfelt dismay mixed in with the shooting pain in her ankle.

'You could have been trampled,' Curtis said and Tessa opened one eye to look at him. For once, there was no smile on his face as he fought his way across the road, belligerently ordering people to stand aside so that he could get through and cursing under his breath.

He briefly allowed her to stand on one foot for the ten seconds it took him to hail a taxi.

There was no point telling him that she was fine and would be able to make it back to her house without help. She wasn't fine. Her foot was killing her. She doubted she would have been able to call a taxi for herself, never mind anything else.

Once in the back of the cab, she managed to wriggle herself into a fairly upright and dignified position and turned to him stiffly.

'Thank you.'

'You're welcome. How does it feel?'

'Awful.' She experimentally tried to move it and winced. It was already beginning to swell and she didn't protest when he gingerly eased it onto his lap so that he could remove her shoe.

'We need to get you to a hospital. Get this properly seen to.'

'No!'

Curtis ignored her, leaning forward to tell the driver to get them to the Kensington and Chelsea Hospital as quickly as he could without killing anyone, then he sat back and reached his hand along her thighs.

'What are you doing?' Tessa yelped, trying to tug her leg away from him but greatly hampered by the pain in her foot every time she moved it. 'Get your hands *off me*!'

'Shh!'

'I will not *shut up*!' Her uncooperative leg refused to sprint off his lap.

'Look,' he said bluntly, 'There will be some gravel, probably, embedded in your ankle and knees where you took the brunt of the fall. With your leg swelling up at the rate it is, the gravel is going to become glued to your tights and it'll be a hell of a job removing them later on. If I could guarantee that we'd be at the hospital quickly, fine, but look at the traffic. It's Christmas and a half-hour drive could end up taking a lot longer.'

Tessa looked out of the window. The traffic was moving like treacle.

'Now I'm not too sure what you think I might get up to in the back of this taxi, but if you want to try and remove your tights yourself, then go ahead. I'll do the gentlemanly thing and look away, shall I?' There was a sharp, bitter edge in his voice that made her wonder whether he had now added the adjective *ridiculous* to the *dull* one he had already attached the minute he had first clapped eyes on her. Maybe he thought it frankly pathetic that she might overestimate her desirability to the extent that he would make a pass for her again. Again and especially in the back seat of a public transport vehicle.

Tessa still made a go of trying to do it herself, but manoeuvring her foot was next to impossible.

'Done trying?' Curtis asked, watching her with detached, cool interest.

By way of answer, Tessa sighed and leant back, closing her eyes so that she didn't have to witness the spectacle of him disrobing her.

Which didn't stop her feeling the slide of his cool fingers along her legs, up past her thighs to her waist, where he gently eased the tights down, pausing and taking extra care when he came to the swollen ankle.

'Mission accomplished,' he said, holding the tights up in one hand. 'You can open your eyes now.' His voice was still edged with suppressed impatience, as was his face when Tessa did open her eyes to look at him. She snatched the tights and stuffed them into her handbag.

'Thanks.' Her legs were still tingling from where he had touched them, even though there had been nothing personal in the touch. 'I'm sorry to be keeping you from…from whatever it was you had planned… There's no need for you to stay with me once we get to the hospital. I know Casualty can be busy at these places, and I'm more than capable of sitting quietly on my own till I get seen to.'

Curtis didn't answer. He had replaced her feet on his lap and he looked at them. Perfect, narrow feet with delicately painted pink toenails. Hardly the sort of feet to be cooped up in tight court shoes, which was what she had been wearing. But then, didn't this woman wear her clothes like a suit of armour? Stiff little suits that stifled every scrap of femininity? Except he knew, didn't he, that take the clothes away and she was highly feminine?

They spent the next twenty minutes in silence, while the cab driver did his best to beat the traffic.

By the time they reached the hospital, Tessa's nerves were fraying badly at the edges. She had never known Curtis to be quite as silent as he had been in the taxi. He wasn't garrulous in the manner of some people who talked even when they had nothing of interest to say. He talked *because* he was interested. It was all part and parcel of his charm, of that bigger-than-average personality that grabbed people and had them hooked and hanging onto every word he uttered.

She let him help her in, stifling the temptation to insist on paying for the taxi herself, considering she was the one who had needed it. As soon as they were through the door, though, she turned to him with a bright smile, trying to ignore the pounding in her ankle.

'Thanks again. I can take it from here.'

'I'm going to help you to that chair over there and then you're to sit down. I'll be ten minutes.'

'Look,' Tessa said, politeness giving way to irritation because she *just didn't want him around her*, 'there's no need.'

He ushered her to the one free spot, still protesting under her breath, and sat her down, then he leaned over her, supporting himself on the metal arms of the chair.

'Don't even think of staging a protest by doing anything. I'll only be a few minutes.'

'This is ridiculous. It's my fault I'm here and I don't feel very happy about...'

Any further protest was stifled as he placed his mouth very firmly over hers, administering one hard, swift kiss that succeeded in removing all power of speech.

'Well, at least there's *something* that can shut you up,' he murmured.

She was still struggling with a mixture of shock, outrage and stupid, uninvited pleasure when he returned, in less time than he had said.

'Right. Come on.'

'Come on *where*?'

'I'm getting you in for a quick look at that foot. Should take a few minutes unless they feel you need an X-ray.'

'But...but *we're queue jumping*!' She squeaked as he lifted her up in one smooth movement and began striding down the corridor, pushing open the double doors at the end with one foot.

'That's a very English response. Don't worry. This doctor is a personal friend of mine and doesn't work on Casualty. You're taking him away from nothing but his regulatory break.'

'Which he probably needs!'

She was relegated to sidelines when, minutes later, she found herself sitting in a room while Curtis and a young, bespectacled doctor discussed her foot, as though she were only rudimentarily attached to it.

The pronouncement was as Curtis had expected. Sprained but not broken. It was bandaged, a prescription for painkillers was given to be taken only as necessary, two on the spot to ease some of the immediate discomfort, and then the two men chatted briefly before she was established in a wheelchair, feeling an absolute fraud.

'I suppose some time today I might be able to stop thanking you.' Tessa forced gratitude into her voice. Of course, he would not allow her to return home on her own. Even though he must have gleaned by now that she didn't actually *want* him around her, he was still insisting on playing the knight in shining armour.

'Why do I get the feeling that it sticks in your throat?' No ready smile in return to her remark. If she was putting him out that much, she thought nastily, then he had been given more than ample opportunity to shed his duties.

'No one likes to think they've made a burden of themselves.'

'And no one likes to think that they're encouraging resentment simply by being humane.'

'No one asked you to be humane!'

'Would you have preferred me to have left you lying in the street? To get on with it?' Curtis snarled.

Tessa offered him a silent profile. She expected him to direct a few more verbal missiles at her, but when the silence lengthened she couldn't resist peeking, just a little. He was staring out of the window and even though she couldn't actually see his face, she could pretty much guess the expression on it. Sheer anger. He had been kind enough to try and break her *dull* routine by inviting her out for a drink, had been *humane* enough to rescue her when she needed help, had in fact pulled a few strings so that she had avoided a five-hour wait in Casualty on a bleak winter's night, and what, he must be thinking, did he get in return? Certainly not the flowery, dewy-eyed declarations of gratitude he had expected.

Tessa could almost feel sorry for him. Except the fact that he was so busy feeling sorry for *her* stuck in her throat and she had to bite back the temptation to hit him right over his egotistic, masculine head. With her perfectly good right arm.

They reached her house and she politely allowed him to help her to the door, even take her inside.

However, extending the gentlemanly routine to making her a cup of coffee and fetching her something to eat while she rested her leg was beyond the bounds. And she didn't want him in her house. Leaving his mark in yet more places for her to have to deal with at a later date.

'That's very kind,' she said from her disadvantaged position on the sofa where he had laid her, 'but I can manage from here. And besides, you don't want to let that taxi driver go. It'll be hell trying to get hold of another one at this time of year.'

He gave her a brief nod and disappeared, leaving her on the sofa to nurse a certain amount of disappointment. Well, he *would* have better things to do than sit around taking care of his secretary because she had been foolish enough to sprain her ankle. Susie's mystery replacement waiting in the wings wouldn't be too overjoyed to find herself sidelined by some woman to whom he felt obligated because she happened to work with him!

'He'll be back in a couple of hours.' Curtis reappeared, a dark, brooding presence by the sitting-room door. 'And there's no point wasting your breath telling me what I should and shouldn't have done.'

'How did you manage to get him to agree to come back for you?' Tessa asked in a small voice.

'Money. Now, I'm going to make you some egg on toast and some tea.' He handed her the remote for the television. 'Watch some TV. It'll take your mind off your foot.'

But not off *him*. Unfortunately. Despite raising the volume on the television, she was still acutely aware of him in the kitchen, rustling something up, handling her cooking utensils. He would have dumped his coat and jacket in the hall, and would have shoved up the sleeves of his faded denim shirt, exposing his strong, muscular forearms. He always had to loosen his clothing when he worked, undo a couple of buttons on his shirt, push up the sleeves, as though being buttoned up stifled his creative genius.

He returned with the promised egg on toast and a pot of tea, all on a tray that he placed on her lap, having first made sure she was comfortable by puffing up the cushions behind her and dragging over a pouffe on which she could rest her legs.

Tessa thanked him and ate, feigning deep concentration on the Christmas programme on the TV, and he let her get away with it, allowing her to think that she might, just might, be able to ignore his presence for the next hour and a half.

She realised how much she had misread his obliging silence when, as soon as she had finished eating, he removed the tray to ask her what time her sister was expected back.

'Tomorrow morning,' Tessa said dryly. 'She's out with a crowd of her college friends and I told her to stay with one of her friends who lives in central London rather than risk trying to find a taxi late at night to bring her back here. I've booked her one for the morning.'

'In which case—' he held out one hand, which Tessa looked at dubiously '—you need to have a bath and I intend to help you.'

'You must be mad!'

'I think I must be…' Curtis muttered under his breath. He leant down and, before she could launch into her routine of shoving him away, he picked her up, ignoring her shrieks and flailing limbs.

The bathroom was very easy to locate, sandwiched next

to the airing cupboard and between the main bedroom and the guest room which, judging from the art on the walls, would belong to Lucy.

'Now,' he said in a steely voice, 'are you going to carry on kicking and screaming, in which case I'll just continue holding you till you tire yourself out, or are you going to be a nice little girl and do what you're told?'

'Put me down!' she snapped.

'Sure. In a minute.' Still carrying her, he clicked the key to the bathroom door, locking them both in, and pocketed it. Tessa let out a howl of outrage.

'How dare you?'

Curtis placed her on the wooden linen basket and stood up, arms folded. 'Don't get into a state, Tessa. I said I would help you have a bath, not get in it with you!'

'I don't need a bath and *I don't need your help*!'

'I'm going to run the bath. You can get out of your clothes. You should be able to do that just fine but you'll need me to help you in, especially as this Victorian bath is so high-sided.'

He began running the bath, tipping bath foam in and testing the temperature with his hand. 'Okay. I take it from the lack of tell-tale rustling that you haven't removed a stick of clothing. If, when the bath is run, you're still glaring at me and trying to pretend that you're comfortable with being grubby, then you'll leave me no choice but to abandon my gentlemanly approach and undress you. On the other hand, you have my word that I'll look away if you undress yourself and leave the bathroom as soon as you're in the water. Deal?'

'Deal? Deal? You've got a nerve, Curtis Diaz! You know that, don't you?' Under the simmering anger, she could feel her heart hammering inside her and her heightened state of awareness was making her limbs go weak,

and it had nothing to do with her sprain. In fact, the tablets had reduced the sharp pain to a bearable discomfort.

'I reckon you've got roughly two minutes,' he answered, with his back still to her.

He meant it! The arrogance of the man left her speechless, but that didn't take away the fact that he meant every word. If she didn't clamber out of her clothes, he would do it for himself. Tessa hurriedly removed her blouse, leaving her bra in place, then, standing on one leg, she shuffled her skirt down, leaving her underwear similarly in place.

He switched off the bath.

'The bra and pants stay on,' Tessa said, folding her arms. 'If they get wet, they get wet. I'll get them off myself once I'm in the water.'

'Fair enough.' He lifted her up, breathing in, catching the mutinous set of her mouth out of the corner of his eye. Also catching the way the bra gaped as he held her, the way he could see the curve of her breast, the hint of her nipple just partially hidden by the lacy fabric. His breathing thickened and he had to tear his eyes forward as he placed her gently in the water and her body was hidden from view by the layer of bubbles.

'Right,' he said roughly, turning away and not looking over his shoulder as he slotted the key back into the door and opened it, 'I'll be back in fifteen minutes. Okay?'

He cleared out of the bathroom as quickly as he could. One more minute in there and he would be in need of a bath himself, an ice-cold one.

What was happening here? he wondered. The woman was not the type he was drawn to. When the work was over and the office door was shut, he liked his women to be fun. He enjoyed the chase, knowing where it would lead, enjoyed the beautiful packaging even though he always knew that he would inevitably get bored with the toy inside. He suspected that if this particular woman was ever chased by him, she wouldn't hesitate to whack him over the head with a hard object, just as he suspected that what was inside the packaging was way too complex for him. Was that why he couldn't take his eyes off her? Because she took challenge to new heights and what red blooded male could ever resist a good challenge?

That, he thought, washing the dishes and keeping an eye on his watch, must be it.

He was whistling as he headed back up to the bathroom, knocking before entering.

The steam from the bath had softened her cheeks and made them pink and the ends of her hair that had dipped into the water were damp strands. She looked all of eighteen.

'You get the bath sheet,' were her first words, issued as a firm command. 'Hold it up and look away. I'll stand up, I can manage that, and I'll wrap the towel around myself and then you can lift me out.'

'Yes, ma'am.' He had enacted many a bath scene in his life and none of them, he thought wryly, had taken on this format. But he obediently did as he was told, fighting off the urge to look, to savour, to rein in his frantic imagination by actually giving it something real to feed on. It physically hurt, it was so difficult.

'Okay,' Tessa said crisply, when the towel was safely around her. 'You can carry me to my bedroom now.' There was just no point pursuing the protesting damsel business. He would just ride roughshod over her if he figured he had to, and she was too vulnerable to allow him to do that, to really invade her privacy by seeing her naked, touching her bare skin. Bad enough having him lift her now with nothing but a towel between them.

The only way she knew how to counterbalance her

screaming nerves was to pretend to be someone else, someone in control, briskly matter-of-fact about what he was doing. And it had been blissful to get clean, to wash off the scraping of dirt on her legs that had penetrated through her sheer tights when she had fallen.

'Feel better?' Curtis asked, sitting her on the edge of the bed and taking a few healthy steps backwards. 'Refreshed? I've brought you up a couple more tablets in case the pain's beginning to kick back in.' He nodded to the table by the head of her bed. Now seemed a very good time to retreat downstairs. He had helped her home, done the whole rescuing-of-the-damsel-in-distress lot. He could watch a little telly while he waited for his taxi to return, leave her up here to get changed, maybe lie down and rest her foot.

He remained where he was, hands thrust into his pockets. The towel had ridden up her thighs and there was no denying that she had very nice thighs. Great legs, in fact, pale and smooth like satin, and very slender.

He cleared his throat. 'I'll be heading downstairs now,' he said. 'Catch up on some award-winning Christmas reruns while I wait for the taxi.'

'Thanks for everything, Curtis,' Tessa said. 'I'd see you to the door but…' She shrugged and gave him a little smile, which he returned.

'Take the tablets.' Nothing left to be said now. He turned, left the room and was about to head downstairs when one more thing occurred to him. In fact, he had meant to ask her while they were in the office, before a series of unexpected events had landed them up here in her house.

He spun round, pushed open the bedroom door and stopped dead in his tracks.

Tessa, on the bed, on all fours, was reaching out for the glass of water and the tablets. The towel, which she had protectively wrapped around her, had slithered to the ground. The moment between them was electric and it seemed to stretch on and on and on.

There was a savage intensity in his blue eyes that made her feel weak because she could read messages there that were firing into her brain and connecting with it in ways she wouldn't have dreamed possible.

When he took a step towards her, she almost moaned. She knew, in every fibre of her being, that she should cover herself up immediately, that she should *want* to.

So why wasn't she yelling at him to leave the room?

Curtis quietly closed the door behind him and that click was like a decision made.

Tessa fell back against the bed, watching, her eyes dark with hunger as he moved towards her.

All these weeks of looking at him from under her lashes, absorbing every little thing about him, and fighting it off because she recognised the dangers, were like nothing now.

She just wanted him to touch her…

CHAPTER SEVEN

TESSA lay down on the bed, drinking Curtis in with her eyes as he walked slowly towards her, finally to sit on the edge of the bed. 'I know,' she said, sitting up so that their faces were only inches apart. 'This is a bad idea. It's madness.'

By way of response, he smoothed his hand along her thigh, curving his fingers over the dewy silk of her buttocks.

'Your foot...' He had wondered whether he would actually be able to speak, whether his vocal cords might not have dried up altogether, but his voice was low and only shook a little.

'Is still sprained.' Tessa tried twisting it and winced. 'It only hurts when I try to move it.' It seemed a little silly to be discussing her foot when she was naked next to him.

Even though the room was dark, with only the side light switched on, she could still make out the fine lines around his eyes, laughter lines, giving his face character.

The realisation that she loved this man, had fallen head over heels with his impossible, unpredictable, utterly mesmerising personality was just something that she accepted. It didn't leap out at her like a bolt from the blue, more revealed itself finally and inexorably. And yes, she should protect herself from him, from getting hurt by him, but hadn't the damage already been done? He had wormed himself deep into the very core of her and pretending that he hadn't wasn't going to make her feel any better. It was a ploy that certainly hadn't worked over the past few weeks.

'You have a beautiful body,' Curtis said thickly, looking down at her and reaching out to cup a breast in his hand. He felt her shudder as he rubbed the pad of his finger over her nipple. It stiffened and the reaction made him draw his breath in sharply.

This was no game. It was nothing like the romps he had had with the women he had dated over the years. He felt suddenly disoriented and when he raised his hand to caress the nape of her neck, it was shaking.

'Your foot...' he murmured roughly. 'I don't think the doctor would advise...'

Tessa lay back, spreading her arms wide, revealing herself to him in a gesture of pure, abandoned trust.

No, she thought, she didn't trust that he wouldn't hurt her. In fact, it was a dead cert that he would. Curtis Diaz wasn't into all those things that came with relationships, proper relationships. But she could only say how she would feel if she carried on denying the truth to herself.

A slow, thick wave was washing over Curtis, making his thinking sluggish. Lying there, she was bewitching. It went way beyond the contours of her body. It was something glimpsed in her eyes, in the soft, suggestive smile curving her lips. She was the perfect combination of woman and child, tempting and cautious at the same time.

His hands were shaking as he began to undo the buttons of his shirt, watching her watching him. He tugged the shirt out of the waistband of his trousers and pulled it off, feeling like a man performing a striptease.

'All I need is some music,' he joked huskily. He hoped to God he wasn't blushing. That was something he had never done in his life before, but right now, the way those eyes were making him feel, he might just be breaking the habit of a lifetime.

The gossip columnists might have overrated his sexual prowess, but Curtis Diaz was no shrinking violet when it came to the fairer sex. He enjoyed the company of women and he enjoyed making love with them. He certainly never felt nervous in their presence but right now, he was as nervous as hell.

She was leaning up on one elbow, half smiling as his hand rested on the top button of his trousers. Instead of wresting them off, however, Curtis squatted down next to the bed so that his eyes were level with hers.

'Do this often, do you?' The clichéd line sounded a little strangled and he was disturbed to find how much he was hanging on for her answer, even though he knew what it would be.

She was an innocent. He had sensed that from the very first. But what if he was wrong? What if she had a secret side? It was known to happen, wasn't it? Secretary by day, stripper by night…?

When he thought about that possibility, his blood seemed to freeze over in his veins.

'You know I don't,' Tessa confessed truthfully. She sighed and stroked the side of his face. 'And I make a particular habit of staying away from my bosses.'

Curtis captured her hand and turned it palm upwards, so that he could press his lips against the soft flesh. With his trousers still on, he joined her in her bed so that he was lying next to her.

'Funnily enough, I make it a policy of separating work from pleasure myself,' he murmured. The temptation was too much. No matter how hard he concentrated on her face, willing himself to rise above this strange, sinking feeling that was enveloping him, he couldn't resist the lure of her breasts. And touching them wasn't enough, not nearly enough. Not when he could lower his head so that he could take one demanding nipple into his mouth and tease it with the wet caress of his tongue. And that breathless groan was enough to draw his hand along her leg, along that smooth thigh, until it made contact with the soft dampness that she offered to him by parting her legs. His finger found the crease that brought forth a gasp of pure pleasure and he rubbed it gently and rhythmically, struggling to control his own pounding arousal.

Take it easy, he told himself, but, when her sweet moistness was enveloping his exploring fingers, that was nigh on impossible.

He reluctantly drew his hand up to her stomach, kissing her when she protested.

'What about conversation?' he murmured, sprinkling little kisses on her mouth and stroking the swell of her breasts.

'Were we talking? I can't remember…' She hooked her hands behind his neck. If she had thought that she could get away with being more agile, she would have, but the dull ache in her foot was just waiting for an opportunity to become a jabbing pain. Right now, being as still as she could manage was pretty much the best idea, but, Lord, what she wouldn't have done to have been able to curl up into him.

'I was telling you that I don't mix business with pleasure either.'

'Despite the exotic flora you've had decorating your office before I came along?'

'What makes you think that you're not as exotic as the rest of them?' Curtis asked, while through his head the disturbing thought took root that she went beyond exotic. She was positively dangerous.

'The mirror?' Tessa touched his lips with the tip of her tongue and he moaned and closed his eyes for the briefest of seconds.

'Then you need to buy yourself a new one,' he muttered inaudibly. Something, somewhere, was telling him that this was getting way out of control, and that that was definitely not good for a man who had always had everything very much under control. He laughed off the uneasy sensation and tilted her head so that he could kiss her neck.

'Are you going to get undressed?' Tessa asked huskily. Their eyes met for a second.

'Making love can be vigorous,' Curtis said, and simply hearing himself say that threw so many graphic pictures into his head that his now painful erection ached even more. 'Vigorous isn't what the doctor ordered for you.'

'Stop worrying about my foot,' Tessa pleaded. 'The tablets have taken care of most of the pain…'

'Which means that you probably wouldn't feel it too much if I hurt you, at least right now, but as soon as those painkillers wear off, you'll be in agony.'

He flipped onto his back, breathing thickly and not knowing quite what was going on with him. He had to remind himself that reining himself in was not a choice, it was a necessity.

Tessa carefully rolled towards him, slowly drawing one leg to cover his, and he looked at her with dark, frustrated hunger.

He had to go. Something deep inside him, some place that had never existed before, was telling him that he had to leave before…before *what?* Before he could no longer put the brakes on his rampaging desires.

He blindly kissed her upturned face, his tongue probing her mouth while one hand sought what it needed to find, the soft, wet bud pulsing for his touch. He felt her shiver.

It sent the last of his coherent thoughts scattering to the four winds. With a stifled groan, he urgently began to explore her body, pinning her arms back and straddling her so that he could devote equal attention to her breasts. He flicked each one with his tongue and, when she twisted beneath him, took first one then the other into his mouth, sucking hard and watching her arched, flushed face with a deep, thrusting satisfaction.

He began to move lower, trailing his tongue along her flat belly, enjoying her rapid breathing. When he looked up, their eyes tangled, hers dark with hunger, his slumberous with the need to satisfy that hunger.

Before he could lower his head to continue his ministrations of her body, she coiled her fingers into his dark hair, tugging him so that he was looking at her once more.

'Curtis…you can't…'

'Can't what, my darling?'

'I've never…'

'Never…what?' Comprehension dawned and with it came another of those destabilising thrusts of pure satisfaction. 'Never been touched down there before…? In the way I mean to touch you…?'

Tessa nodded. He saw the apprehension in her eyes and his heart did something funny inside him, then he broke eye contact so that he could kiss his way down past her belly button, pausing only for a fraction of a second to breathe in the sweet femininity of her. He blew gently on the soft pubic hair, but the need to taste her was just too overpowering. The musky scent had filled his nostrils and he wanted more, much more.

And tasting her was every bit as good as he had imagined it would be. He could feel her bucking against him, writhing, and he stilled her growing need by flattening his hands on either side of her thighs.

Her groans had increased by several octaves, sweet music to his ears, and as his tongue slid remorselessly over that tightened bud, the essence of her naked hunger, he felt her reach her inexorable climax, arching back, shuddering and finally coming down in restless waves from the peak.

Her eyes were slumberous when he edged himself up so that he was lying next to her.

'That wasn't quite what I had in mind,' she whispered, drawing him to her with drowsy contentment, 'but it felt… well…' Modesty deprived her of voicing a suitable description and Curtis smiled.

With reality weaving its tentacles around him, that uneasy, dangerous feeling was back, although he couldn't put his finger on where it came from.

'I should go…' he murmured.

'But…'

'But you need to get some rest, and, Lord knows, the taxi's probably come and gone.'

Shouldn't he want to stay with her? Tessa suddenly felt very vulnerable. She consoled herself with the thought that she was a modern woman and there was absolutely nothing wrong in fulfilling her needs, especially with the man she loved. Even though he didn't love her back. Still…she pulled the duvet cover from one side to partially cover her exposed body.

When he heaved himself off the bed, the vulnerability feeling grew stronger. This time she swamped herself under the duvet and pushed herself into a sitting position, leaning back against the headboard so that she could watch him as he slipped back on his shirt and slowly began doing up the buttons.

'I never got to mention why I came back into your room,' Curtis said roughly. 'I meant to ask whether you and your sister would like to come over on Boxing Day.

Anna wants to see you and it makes even more sense now that you probably won't be able to do very much with your foot.' He grinned crookedly at her. She looked so damned edible lying there, all bundled up under that duvet. His hands itched to rip it away but he knew that if he did, he would be lost, would end up never wanting to leave. No, he corrected uncomfortably, not wanting to leave in a hurry...

He took one step back, as though he had been standing too close to an open fire, and then turned at the sound of the doorbell.

'Your taxi awaits you,' Tessa said.

'Hang on. I'll just tell him that I'll be down in a minute.'

'It's Christmas. He may not be prepared to wait that long.'

It was suddenly chilly in the room the minute he vacated it. In fact, it had become pretty chilly in the bed the second he had got out, but there was no point moaning about what had happened or about the fact that she felt a great deal more vulnerable now than she had before.

She had wanted him. She had wanted to feel his big body next to hers. Just thinking about it now made her shiver.

And she was a realist, wasn't she? Had she really expected declarations of love in the heat of passion? The cold clutch of uncertainty gripped her and she fought it off, listening for the sound of his footsteps approaching.

When she finally did hear him, she felt her body tense.

'No taxi,' Curtis said, standing by the door for a few moments before coming into the room and gently pushing the door shut behind him. 'I phoned for another, but there's a waiting list, apparently, as long as the Great Wall of China.'

'Then who was it at the door?' Tessa asked, forgetting what he had said about the non-appearing taxi.

'Your sister.'

'Oh!' She froze while a thousand possible scenarios raced through her head like a swarm of bees. 'Oh. I thought...I wasn't expecting her to come home until tomorrow,' Tessa said breathlessly.

'Seems she decided that an all-night drinking binge wasn't such a good idea.'

'Oh, right.' She looked anxiously at Curtis, wondering how to phrase the unavoidable question, but in all events he read her mind and answered it without having to be asked.

'I told her that you had sprained your ankle and I had done the good employer thing and brought you back. I told her that you were up in bed, nicely settled, and that I was on my way out.'

What did you think of her? Tessa wanted to ask him, but she bit back the temptation. Instead, she said, 'I must get up and go down to see her.'

'Don't be ridiculous. Your foot needs rest. The last thing you want to do is leap down the stairs to make sure your sister is all right. Trust me, she's fine.'

'I wasn't planning on leaping anywhere!' Tessa retorted. 'Would you mind passing me some clothes if I tell you where to find them?' Before he could answer, she was pointing to her chest of drawers, directing him towards her underwear, a long-sleeved tee shirt and her most comfortable pair of jogging bottoms. All items of clothing that the fashion police would have her hung, drawn and quartered for wearing, but she needed to get changed quickly, something that she did with his help. Lord, but it was difficult, when her body kept having a mind of its own and, as much as she kept hurrying him up, so he took his time. She protested but could hardly prevent the groundswell of excitement every time his fingers brushed against her skin.

Once she was fully dressed, she informed him that he could take her down.

'Would that be a command?' he asked, amused at the change between the woman with clothes on and the woman with them off.

'I could always try and go it on my own.'

'I take that back. It wasn't a command. It was a cunning piece of emotional blackmail.'

He lifted her up and carried her down the stairs while she protested futilely on what her sister would say.

Lucy, as it turned out, said nothing for a few seconds. She just looked as Curtis brought Tessa in and deposited her on the sofa.

'I see you've been swept off your feet, sis!' Lucy's face broke into a smile of pure charm and she flashed Curtis an approving look.

It was the sort of look that inspired jealousy in other females. Tessa had never, ever, been jealous of her sister. She had been proud of the lovely child who had matured into a gorgeous adult. Lucy had all the hallmarks of the glamorous bimbo. Long, streaming blonde hair, perfectly chiselled features, wide blue eyes and a figure that screamed out for very tight clothing. However, she was saved from being the archetypal blonde by nature of her personality. Her eyes danced and her mouth looked as though it was permanently ready to laugh. There was something sweetly wicked about her and it had got men hooked time and time again.

No, Tessa had become used to sitting back and enjoying her sister's impact.

Not quite so now. She couldn't bring herself to look at Curtis just in case he, too, was falling under her sister's spell.

She caught herself. This was the man who had just made

love to her! Touched her in ways that had set her body alight!

But then…a little voice of malice said, he hadn't exactly been shouting out his love, had he? Or even his attraction. And it hadn't really been *making love*, had it? Not really. Not technically. He had pleasured her…

Lucy had flopped into one of the chairs, with one leg dangling over the arm and her head thrown back.

She was managing to turn brown into a colour everyone might conceivably want to wear, in the hope that they might pull it off too. Brown, flared jeans, brown tight cardigan cropped at the waist, exposing a terracotta-coloured silk vest. Nothing else. No jewellery, nothing brash, just utter simplicity.

Tessa roused herself sufficiently to answer Lucy's questions about how she fell and where and how and why and wasn't she so lucky to have had her boss there, on the spot, ready to charge into action and rescue her from being trampled to death by crowds of people intent on Christmas shopping.

Lucy made a feeble attempt at a joke about Christmas, turkeys and shoppers, forgetting the punchline three times, but still managed to evoke a hearty chuckle from Curtis when she did finally remember. Tessa's laugh was a little more forced.

'You seem pretty sober for a night on the tiles, Luce,' she said, changing the subject from herself, and Lucy snorted, sitting up straighter and tucking her legs under her.

'Started too early,' she explained. 'Lunch time, in fact. Just a quick one at the pub and you know how it goes. I barely drank a thing, actually. I'd planned on doing a bit of, yes, shopping, and I spent half my time checking my watch and wondering whether I could leave and catch them all up a bit later. Which is what I did, except by the time

I caught them up I was as sober as a judge and they were rolling in the aisles.'

'Not a good situation,' Curtis said sympathetically. Tessa's acidity levels rose accordingly. The warm glow she had felt in the immediate aftermath of their love-making was fading fast. Too many doubts had set in, and now, when she sneaked a look at Curtis, it was to find his attention focused on her sister.

'Hence,' Lucy was saying airily, 'my early night. Well, early compared to what I had planned on. I would have come home a lot sooner if I had known about your leg, sis.' Her voice became serious. 'You should have called me.'

'I didn't think you'd hear your phone amid the noise,' Tessa hedged. Actually, calling her sister hadn't occurred to her at any point in time. Why would it? she thought sourly. How many damsels in distress would choose being rescued by a disgruntled sibling dragged away from a hell raising pre-Christmas pub-crawl over a knight in shining armour? Especially when said damsel in distress was in love with the knight in question?

'True,' Lucy admitted readily enough. 'Although it does vibrate. I would have felt it in my bag. Maybe. Well, much more fun being rescued by a tall, gorgeous hunk, anyway.' She giggled and Curtis shot Tessa a look that very much resembled a cat in possession of the proverbial cream.

'Oh, good grief,' Tessa said, 'that sort of remark is just the thing to go to his head. Which,' she added, 'is already heavily inflated anyway.'

'Though not by your sister, I hasten to assure you,' Curtis addressed Lucy, who gave them both an odd little look from under her lashes. 'So…' he leaned back and relaxed '…I've heard enough about you. Tell me what you do, Lucy.'

Tessa butted in before this particular conversation could kick off. 'Shouldn't you be thinking of leaving, Curtis? I mean, taxis...Christmas...long wait...'

'Oh, I'll drop him back! If you'll let me borrow your car, Tess. I can guarantee that the alcohol levels in my blood are non-existent, despite original plans.' She giggled and Tessa frowned, not liking this suggestion but not really knowing how she could deflect the inevitable acceptance of the offer from Curtis.

Jealousy ate away like a poison and she knew why. Lucy was just the sort of girl Curtis went for.

When she tried to tell herself that he had slept with *her,* had made love to *her*, the little nasty voice she was becoming accustomed to reminded her that she had been the one to put temptation in his way, that he was a commitment-free zone who hadn't once mentioned anything normal like, When shall we meet again? On a date? She, the little voice continued remorselessly, had wanted him because she felt more than mere physical attraction. He, on the other hand, was the same person who had felt sorry for her and still did.

In the middle of her protracted internal debates, she was aware of Curtis quizzing Lucy about her course, asking her a million questions about the kind of things she designed, on what she intended to do once she was through with college. As usual, intently curious, leaning forward with his elbows resting on his thighs, his amazing eyes focused on Lucy's face as she spoke, his head inclined in the attitude of the avid listener. Pure animal magnetism flowed off him in waves. The sort of waves that women could easily drown in.

Lucy, enjoying the single-minded attention, was happily talking about Lucy and Tessa noticed that she seemed to be a heck of a lot more forthcoming about her possible future with him than she was with her. None of her usual vague 'oh, I'll just wait and see what happens when the course is finished' nonsense. Oh, no. Apparently she had ideas of going into advertising! Starting at the bottom and working her way up the ladder!

Tessa sourly thought that a few magic words of interest from Curtis Diaz and suddenly her sister was a miracle of revelation.

'I think I'll be heading up now.' She yawned and they both looked at her. 'Sorry if I'm spoiling the party,' she muttered and Curtis threw her an amused smile.

'I'll carry you up, m'lady.' He stood up and bowed lavishly to Lucy's merriment and Tessa's annoyance.

'It's okay. You've already done enough, thanks. I'll try and make my own way upstairs. I think I should get as much practice using this foot anyway. It's not as though it's broken or anything.'

'Don't be ridiculous. Treat that foot properly and you'll be ready for dancing in a couple of days' time. Walk on it and you'll end up laid up for the next two weeks.'

'Which would be fine considering I won't have to go to work,' Tessa retorted, standing up and delicately placing a bit of pressure on the foot in question.

Before she was aware of it, he was next to her and sweeping her up in one easy movement. Out of the corner of her eye, Tessa could see her sister grinning like a Cheshire cat and she scowled, unfortunately into Curtis's chest.

She couldn't work out where things had all gone so horribly wrong. The feel-good factor that had been there in the bedroom, the sensation that everything she was doing, mad though it all was, was somehow *right* had disappeared like a puff of smoke.

What had she done? Bit late in the game to start asking

questions like that, she thought, but they still kept coming at her thick and fast and Curtis, with his usual impeccable perception, had obviously clocked into that because as soon as he deposited her on the bed he stood back, arms folded, every inch the forbidding male.

'What's the matter with you?' he asked her without preamble.

'Matter?'

'Don't play dumb, Tessa.'

Tessa decided to drop the act. She had never been very good at playing dumb anyway. She shrugged and went for the outright lie instead. 'I didn't want to say anything but my foot was beginning to act up a little.' She looked at it mournfully. The painkillers were doing a brilliant job. 'You were right. It needs to be rested if it's to mend.' Curtis being a man, she thought that that little piece of ego flattery would deflect him from his perceptive appraisal of her mood, which was something she didn't want to dwell on.

'Sweet of you to agree with me on that one.'

Tessa's eyes flickered to his face. His expression was serious but there was just enough of an edge of sarcasm to his voice to make her think that the syrupy appeal to his male ego hadn't been as accurate as she had hoped.

'So, what do you think of Lucy?' she asked, idly brushing some non-existent fluff from her jogging bottoms. Her body tensed. To have not asked the question would have spared her any unwanted truths but she knew that she had to find out. For her own peace of mind. She wasn't looking at him but she could almost hear him thinking.

'Not what I expected.'

'What did you expect?'

'Someone a lot more frivolous.'

But you found her attractive, didn't you? Tessa wanted

to press on. In other words, you were attracted to her, weren't you? In ways you could never be attracted to me?

'She's got some interesting things to say. Would you like to look at me when I'm talking?'

'Sorry. Just a little sleepy, that's all.' I have a stunningly attractive, deep and interesting sister. More silly, foolish, unfamiliar, unacceptable jealousy seared through her. She wanted to point out that, gorgeous and interesting though she might be, she hadn't invented a cure for cancer, for goodness' sake! 'What?' she asked irritably, because he looked as though he was about to say something.

'It's nothing,' he said eventually. 'You're tired. You need to get to sleep.' He stepped towards her, undeterred by the wall of frost she had erected, and sat on the bed next to her. When he lowered his head to gently kiss her on the lips, she wanted to pull back. Pride should have made her pull back. But the pressure of his mouth was so sweet, so unbearably sweet, that she closed her eyes and kissed him gently back. And hated herself for it the minute her eyes were open again and he was back by the door, lounging against it and eyeing her with brooding speculation. The kind of brooding speculation that made her wonder what exactly he was thinking and what he had been on the verge of saying to her before he changed his mind.

For someone who could be flamboyantly open, he possessed a talent for self-concealment, she thought uneasily.

Catching herself thinking and staring, Tessa made a show of yawning widely before snapping off the bedroom light and rolling onto her side.

He left quietly, without shutting the bedroom door. The corridor light will keep me up, she thought, but the effort of doing something about it was too much. Besides, now that she was lying down, she discovered that she really was tired. Exhausted from the battle that had been raging inside her.

She expected to hear the sound of the front door any minute, but in fact she nodded off before the anticipated click came and only awoke, groggily, some time later. She didn't know how much later because she had left her watch on the dressing table.

She was only aware of two things. The sound of voices from below and an urgent need to go to the bathroom.

Her foot had stiffened up and was aching, but it struck Tessa that it was amazing how Nature's setbacks could be circumnavigated provided the incentive was right.

In this case, the incentive was her burning curiosity to find out what was being said at the bottom of the stairs.

Shouldn't Lucy have dropped him off and be back home by now? Because, even though she couldn't discern the words, she could instantly recognise the timbre of Curtis's voice.

She hobbled to the door, pulled it slightly wider and then dropped to all fours. Ludicrous but necessary. If she walked, or rather staggered, to the top of the stairs, they would both notice her, unless they coincidentally had their backs both turned. They would see her the minute she emerged from behind the wall, from which the staircase down went directly to the small hallway.

On the other hand, it would be highly unlikely that they would notice if she just peered round the wall at ground level.

She slithered into position, peeped and saw Lucy and Curtis both by the front door, which was open. Through it Tessa could see the back end of a taxi. He had somehow managed to find one. That momentary distraction didn't last long.

They were making no attempt to keep their voices low,

obviously expecting her to be well away in the land of Nod, so she didn't have to strain to hear what was being said.

All the usual pleasantries. And they didn't appear to be standing too close to one another. Tessa wondered whether she had mistakenly jumped to wrong conclusions. Her mind was halfway wandering off, dreaming up impossible scenarios, when he said it, appropriately dropping his voice to a lower decibel.

'So are you sure it's okay if I get in touch with you...?'

Lucy laughed and pinkened. 'Absolutely.' She tiptoed and kissed him demurely on his cheek. Tessa's heart, which was in full plummet, fell even further. 'I never thought when I came home tonight that I would end up meeting someone who could turn out to be so good for me!'

From where he was standing, with his hand on the door, he smiled, and Tessa squeezed her eyes shut very tightly, fighting back the tears of self pity.

'But not a word to your sister. Not yet. I thought of saying something when I said goodnight to her, but let's just see where we're going with this before...before, well, we say anything...'

'I agree.'

'And I'll see the both of you on Boxing Day!'

Tessa didn't wait to hear the remainder of the damning conversation. She crawled back to her bedroom, hobbled to the bathroom and practically sprinted to her bed before Lucy could make it up the stairs and discover that her sister was still up.

Although, Tessa thought bitterly, no girlish sharing of confidences would be forthcoming. Not when there was so much to hide...

One thing she knew for sure...she would not be going to spend Boxing Day with him. No way was she going to witness Lucy and Curtis flirting surreptitiously with one another while she skulked in the corner with various assorted relatives, pretending that everything was fine and dandy!

CHAPTER EIGHT

CHRISTMAS DAY was a miserable, protracted affair that involved a great deal of jaw-aching jollity as Tessa pretended that everything was all right. In the absence of any other family members, they had always made a big thing of Christmas lunch, making sure that all the trimmings were there, from the traditional turkey to the mince pies. With her foot still too sore to handle the cooking, Tessa watched as Lucy took over, displaying nerve-jangling cheeriness as she flitted across the kitchen, keeping up a steady stream of conversation. It would have been too much if there had been just the two of them over the Christmas lunch, but thankfully three of Lucy's friends, all Australians who were over for the duration of the course, joined them for lunch and, from the relative safety of onlooker, Tessa felt free to observe her sister undercover.

Was it her imagination or did Lucy seem to be over-bright? She was like a wind-up toy into which new batteries had been inserted. Tessa thought that her sister could have continued for days, chattering and laughing and brimming over with gaiety. It was infectious. At least for the guests. Never flat at the best of times, the Australians were positively bursting with good cheer.

At seven, Tessa could stand it no longer and made her excuses. A headache, she apologised, avoiding Lucy's probing, concerned eyes. As excuses went, it was pretty feeble, but it could prove useful in the morning when she pulled it back out of her hat and produced it as a reason why she couldn't possibly go to any Boxing Day thing at the Diaz residence.

Purely to avoid a confrontation on Christmas Day, Tessa had allowed her sister to assume that their little outing on Boxing Day was a foregone certainty. A so-called headache accompanied by a weak smile would at least give her some warning that ill health was destined to make an appearance first thing in the morning.

'I'll walk you up.' Lucy shot to her feet, all worried concern.

'No need. You…you stay here with…your friends. I'm more than capable of making it up some stairs without hurtling down backwards!' She gently tried to prise her arm out of her sister's grasp. Just the feel of those treacherous fingers on her made her want to recoil in misery.

But none of this was her sister's fault. She had told herself this over and over again. Lucy had had no idea that she and Curtis were involved. As far as she was concerned, she wasn't treading on any toes. Curtis was up for grabs and he had clearly not seen fit to enlighten her. The blame lay fully at his door.

Still…Tessa couldn't bring herself to look at her sister so she remained staring glassily at the assembled trio still sitting down, who stared back at her with varying degrees of intoxication.

'What on earth is *the matter with you*?' Lucy hissed, tugging her towards the door, one hand around her waist. 'You've been acting very strange today.'

'Have I?' Tessa muttered. She wondered how Lucy would react if she started pouring out what was in her head. Of course, she wasn't going to do that. Not now, not ever. Opening up those particular dam gates would be a very bad idea. For a start, she would end up having to confess why it hurt so much, having to admit that she had fallen head over heels in love with a man whose feelings towards her were casual at best. Her sister would be horrified. God, she would probably join the Pity Crew, of whom Curtis Diaz was a platinum-card member!

'You know you have! You've barely said a word all day! And after I slaved over a hot stove cooking up Christmas lunch for us!'

'Poor Lucy,' Tessa said unsympathetically. 'Awful having to take care of yourself for a change, isn't it? Not to mention, take care of me as well!'

'I was just joking, Tess.'

'Well, I'm not. I'm tired and my head hurts and I want to go to bed.' She debated whether she should just go for it and inform her sister that the headache would still be ongoing in the morning so she could squash any idea of her trudging over to the Diaz place for Boxing Day frivolities.

'Okay,' Lucy said hurriedly, 'but I'll get you some painkillers and I have something here...' She fumbled in one of her pockets and extracted a small silver object, which she handed to her sister. 'It's a whistle,' she explained sheepishly. 'No single girl is complete without one.'

Tessa took it and turned it over in her hand. 'I know what it is, Lucy. I'm just wondering what I'm supposed to do with it.'

'You're supposed to blow it every time you need me.' They had reached the bedroom and Lucy turned so that the sisters were facing one another. 'Just in case I've not got round to saying this, Tess...I'm really grateful for everything you've done for me since Mum and Dad died... and...well, all the stuff you're still doing now. I know I've been hard work in the past...'

Some of the frozen ice in Tessa's heart melted. Or maybe

just got redistributed to the ice block weighted against Curtis.

'I'm so used to seeing you up and about in control of everything that…it's been salutary to know that you can be as helpless as anybody else…'

'What do you mean *helpless*?' Tessa feverishly scanned back to how she had behaved throughout the course of the day. Quiet, yes, but had she come across as *helpless*? Had she been that transparent? She felt her face blanch, which increased Lucy's level of sibling concern, and she found herself gently propelled into the bedroom and onto the bed.

'Well, *ill*, you know…' Lucy said awkwardly, looking across from where she was rummaging in her sister's drawer for a nightdress. 'Not physically able to do the caring thing that you normally do so well.' She handed the nightdress to Tessa, unable to resist commenting on the baggy nature of it.

'I like baggy,' Tessa said, allowing some help with the process of getting undressed and then lying back on the pillows once she was in the baggy, thigh-length nightie with its Tigger motto.

Already sensitive to the unfolding nightmare between Lucy and Curtis, she mentally added a postscript to this statement. She liked baggy but men didn't. Men liked women like Lucy, sexy women who wore sexy lingerie. Not that her sister favoured the kind of lacy jobs that were touted as sexy. More little strappy cotton vests and very brief briefs, which were perfect at tantalisingly showing up every inch of skin.

'So what did you think of Curtis?' Tessa asked, not meaning to but unable to help herself. She noticed the brightness in her sister's eyes when the name was mentioned, as though someone had lit a lightbulb inside her.

Just the way *she* had felt whenever he was around, Tessa thought painfully.

'Very dishy.' Lucy pretended to sigh but her eyes were still bright and excited when she glanced at her sister. 'Don't you think?'

Tessa shrugged. 'He's all right, I suppose, if you go for that kind of thing.'

Her heart clenched painfully even though her voice was perfectly modulated, even dismissive. If Lucy ever found out about the two of them, she would be appalled, but Tessa was quite sure that Curtis wouldn't breathe a word. Even a fool would know that to spill those particular beans would be the death knoll of any burgeoning relationship and Curtis was no fool. Not by a long shot.

'It's not just the way he looks.' Lucy looked seriously at her sister. 'I mean, he's good looking enough, but...he's...well, I just get the feeling that he's one of the good guys...'

Which shows how savvy you are when it comes to members of the opposite sex, Tessa thought. She closed her eyes, feigning exhaustion, and was pleased when her sister immediately took the hint.

The headache she had pretended now really did feel as though it was coming on. Her temples throbbed and her eyes were hurting from unshed tears. She finally drifted off to sleep with snatches of overheard conversation providing a rich foundation for a series of disturbing, disjointed dreams in which she pursued a faceless couple who disappeared out of reach whenever they came within touching distance.

She woke up at a little before nine, feeling as though she hadn't slept at all. The same snatches of conversation that she had gone to bed contemplating resumed their relentless torture and not even the laborious process of having a bath and thinking about what to wear could push them to one side.

She emerged from the bathroom to find Lucy waiting for her, along with an immaculately prepared breakfast tray, complete with a flower in a vase.

'You should have blown the whistle,' Lucy said, frowning. 'That's why I gave it to you. You blow and I come. Still. Never mind. Look, I've made you breakfast. Am I or am I not the perfect sister? Toast, scrambled eggs, juice, coffee…' She hovered like a sergeant major, watching as Tessa made her way over to the chair by the window, then she deposited the nicely arranged tray on her lap.

'Course, you'll have to gulp it down.' She folded her arms and waited in expectation that her sister would obey orders. 'I told Curtis that we'd be over by eleven, in time for some pre-lunch drinks, which leaves…' she looked at her watch and did some mental arithmetic '…a little over an hour and you know how long it takes me to get going.'

'My headache…' Tessa made a wincing gesture and tucked into the breakfast, head downturned just in case Lucy spotted the little white lie. 'I don't think I'm going to be able to make it. My head…and my foot…I'd be better off resting up… But you go!' The false brightness in her voice threatened to overspill into tears. She would have to watch that.

'I can't go on my own!' Lucy's voice was horrified. 'You *have* to come, Tess!'

'Have to? I don't think so.' When she glanced up at her sister, she saw that Lucy was stricken. *Stricken!* One hour in the man's company and she was already distraught at the thought of not seeing him! 'You'll be fine without me,' she said coolly. 'Face it, Luce, you've never needed me around to hold your hand when it came to dealing with the opposite sex.'

'You don't understand. Anyway, staying here will be horrible and grim and depressing. What will you do? Hang around watching television in your Tigger nightie?'

Sounded fine to Tess.

'He might think that you're annoyed with him for some reason,' Lucy continued with a shrewdness that Tessa would never have expected.

It did make her think, though.

Lucy had a point. If she chickened out, Curtis would immediately come to the conclusion that he had offended her, and, since she was determined to emerge from her ill-conceived race into bed with him with dignity, showing any sign of offence was number one on the forbidden list.

Also, Curtis was unpredictable. He didn't obey conventions. She wouldn't put it past him to come to the house and confront her. If there was one thing Tessa knew she couldn't handle, it was that. She shuddered over the remainder of her toast and egg and hurriedly gulped down a mouthful of coffee.

'He probably wouldn't even notice my absence,' she said lamely, and Lucy made a stern tut-tutting noise under her breath.

'False modesty and you know it!' She removed the tray from her sister's lap. 'You just have to come. Now, what are you going to wear?'

'Why is it so important for us to go, Luce?' The question was innocent enough but Tessa's eyes narrowed speculatively on her sister's face, which reddened. The most conclusive sign of guilt Tessa could imagine. Her heart hardened. It was a good job Curtis Diaz wasn't around, she thought bitterly. Her famed composure might have undergone some serious fracturing. Along with his head.

'I thought I might take along some of my work,' Lucy

said, her colour deepening. 'Curtis seemed very interested in the sort of stuff I'm doing at the moment.'

'Oh, did Curtis?'

The inveterate charmer, she thought, her heart clenching. Always showed interest in other people and not just mild curiosity, but real interest. Or so it seemed. Poor Lucy. If she could have warned her, she would have, but she could hardly admit to speaking from experience and, besides, when it came to men, Lucy was a law unto herself.

But there were other ways of warning...

She stood up. Her foot, after that initial day of pain, was already strong enough to take some of her weight, though not comfortably. She still allowed herself to be helped to the bathroom and while she was doing her usual morning routine, even allowed Lucy to rifle through her wardrobe and choose some clothes for her to wear.

The choice was a pair of sand-coloured cord trousers, a similarly coloured roll-necked jumper and Lucy had completed the ensemble with a Burberry scarf of her own and a tan jacket, also hers, which fashionably came to mid-thigh. In terms of combating winter cold, it wasn't very practical but it did look very fetching. Besides, Tessa didn't have the energy to complain. Her energy was all being used up by the tide of emotions running amok inside her. There was just none left to distribute anywhere else.

They arrived at the Diaz house promptly at eleven, a minor miracle considering Lucy never arrived anywhere on time.

An intimate family gathering was Tessa's greatest fear, and her fear was misplaced because they arrived to find a throng of guests. Family members, of which there were many, mixed alongside old family friends and various members of *their* family. And, of course, Anna was there, ready to usher them in.

In one corner of the enormous room stood the most impressive Christmas tree Tessa had ever seen. It stretched from floor to ceiling and glittered with tiny white lights and what looked like an entire Harrods department's worth of stunning baubles, all in various shades of cream and ivory.

And lounging by the tree in a group was Curtis, dressed in his usual unique way. Faded jeans and a jumper with an off-puttingly elaborate pattern of reindeer. He saw her as soon as she walked through the door and Tessa felt that electric feeling of primitive awareness, as though her body had suddenly become alive. She smiled stiffly and then turned her attention back to Anna, asking her a thousand questions about her work at school and how she was getting on, whether her brief stint at filing was proving useful.

'Very!' Anna said, grinning. 'Now I just file away anything I don't like the look of, straight into the bin by my dressing table.'

'Well, somcthing useful *did* come out of your working stint,' Tessa said teasingly, 'aside from that valuable filing art. Look at you! Very trendy. I recognise the top. Isn't that the one we got in that little boutique by the shoe shop?'

'Yes. The one Dad thought was a little too tight and a little too colourful and a little too…unwearable for his precious daughter!' Anna laughed. 'Mr Pot decides to call Miss Kettle black. I mean, look at him…' Her voice was soft with affection. 'He's the only one who would dare come to a do like this dressed in a pair of his oldest jeans and that jumper! A present from one of his ex-girlfriends, apparently.'

Tessa thought that she would rather not look at him, but she did anyway. The magnetic pull of his personality from across the room was just too much to bear. And besides, she and Anna were now being descended upon by various other people, Curtis's brother, Mark, his wife, and a delicate, elderly lady who seemed to be a godmother to one of the boys. Tessa smiled and went onto autopilot when they asked her about her foot, which was in an endearing bedroom slipper, but her eyes strayed over to Curtis. Now, the little group that had surrounded him had disbanded. In their place was an animated Lucy, cheeks flushed, glass of champagne jiggling precariously as she talked and gesticulated. Like someone who had known him for years instead of the perfect stranger that she was. The portfolio that she had lugged over was nowhere in evidence and Tessa assumed that it had been dumped somewhere, that it had been no more than a plausible excuse for Lucy's real reason for wanting to make it over here.

Jovial conversation continued to swim around her as she looked furtively at the chatting couple by the Christmas tree. Now Lucy must have said something about the tree, because she leant forward and gently touched one of the baubles, twirling it in her fingers.

She was dressed perfectly for the occasion. A deep burgundy skirt reaching to mid-calf and a small, long-sleeved top in a matching colour with a neckline designed to discreetly attract attention to what God had so generously given her up top. She had pinned up her long fair hair in an untidy pony-tail and a few artful strands danced around her cheeks as she leant forward to admire the bauble on the tree.

'Great tree,' Tessa said, looking away. 'Must have taken for ever to decorate.' She took time out to look at Curtis's brother, who was clearly older and far more traditional than his younger sibling. He was also fairer, without the dramatic looks that Curtis possessed. An affable, charming man married to an elegant woman with two very good-looking children, both under the age of five. Tessa drank her first glass of champagne, decided that it was doing wonders for her spirits and accepted another from the tray that was being passed around by a young girl in uniform.

She had almost convinced herself that she had forgotten about Curtis's presence in the room, when she felt a soft tap on her shoulder and looked around to find him smiling down at her, telling her that her foot would be the size of a beach ball if she continued standing on it for much longer.

'Don't worry.' He grinned at his brother. 'I'll make sure she doesn't want for drinks, nibbles or amusing company.'

They were friends, Tessa thought, not merely two men who happened to share the same gene pool. The look that passed between them was full of mutual affection. A bit like she and Lucy. She automatically glanced around and saw that Lucy was being Lucy with two elderly gentlemen.

'There's no need to treat me like an invalid,' Tessa said in a prickly voice. 'My foot's actually a lot better. It must have been a very minor twist.' She was acutely aware of his long fingers curled around her forearm as he led her towards one of the deep chairs in the corner of the room. 'How was your day yesterday? It must have been marvellous sitting under that tree opening presents!' Her voice was high and light and stunningly polite.

'Oh, marvellous.' He pulled up a footstool and perched on it, one arm resting lightly on the arm of her chair. 'I was up at three in the morning, of course, all excited at what Santa might have brought for me.' He grinned, inviting her to share his amusement, and Tessa looked back at him blankly.

When she thought of his little tête à tête with her sister, when she imagined the sizzling lust that must have sprung into life the minute he'd clapped eyes on Lucy, just the thought of sharing any kind of joke with him made her feel physically sick. But she still held onto her smile.

'And what *did* you get?' she asked politely. He had positioned his body in such a way that he effectively blocked out the rest of the circulating party. Most of the older people had found chairs for themselves and were catching up on a year's worth of anecdotes. Mark and Emily's two children were whizzing round the room, with Anna in attendance, and Lucy had moved on to another group with the effortless ease of the born mixer.

'This magnificent jumper from an ex-girlfriend of long ago who's now happily married with a child and apparently thinks I need taking care of in the way of clothing. I like it.' He plucked at it and made a show of trying to make sense of the gaudy pattern.

'It's very cheerful.'

'Which is more than can be said about you,' Curtis said, with his usual lack of preamble. His blue eyes took on a wicked glint and Tessa quickly looked away.

'Yes, well…I didn't sleep all that well with my foot…'

'Which you said was definitely on the mend…'

'On the mend but not quite there yet,' Tessa informed him irritably, knowing that the foot was the last thing that had disturbed her sleep patterns.

'Lucy said you went to bed early with a headache,' Curtis remarked, and Tessa flinched at the intimacy implied in discussing her behind her back.

'Your brother's very nice.' She changed the conversation abruptly and cast her eyes around him, scanning the room and hopefully giving off signals of restlessness. 'He was telling me all about his house in Scotland and what it's like living there…'

'Riveting stuff.' Curtis's eyes were narrowed speculatively on her face. 'Ground-breaking social repartee, I would say.'

'I'd like to go and meet your mother.' Tessa dodged the verbal missile that she knew was designed to stimulate a response in her. As was his body language, leaning into her, elbows resting on his thighs. When did he plan to tell her about Lucy? she wondered. Once she had been eased gently off the scene? 'She's caught my eye a couple of times. I must seem very rude coming here and then ignoring the hostess.'

'I shouldn't worry about it.' Curtis could feel his irritation growing as she glanced across the room, cleverly avoiding the blue eyes that were trying to pin her down. 'Right now, Mum's as busy as the proverbial bee. It's the same every Boxing Day. Mark and I tell her just to do something light and trouble free, beg her to get the caterers in…'

'And…?' Tessa reluctantly looked at him, charmed by the evident love in his voice when he discussed the members of his family.

'And she agrees wholeheartedly. All through the month of November. At which point she begins letting slip the odd remark that people always preferred home-cooked food instead of all that plastic perfection that caterers were so good at, that *light food* was fine but that it had to be *interesting light food*. Then Boxing Day arrives and she's rushed off her feet, even though Anna does her best to try and help out. Despite the distractions…' They both looked at his daughter, who was now involved in amateurishly face-painting one of his brother's children.

'You let her wear the clothes she bought in London,' Tessa couldn't help remarking. 'She looks beautiful.'

'You can take the credit for that,' Curtis said lazily. 'Actually, you did me a favour. I was a little overprotective, thought I could keep her in strait-laced frocks suitable for the over forties when actually she would have asserted herself sooner or later. Better she asserted herself when she happened to be with you than later on, in the company of someone her own age with a taste for provocative clothing.'

'Or Lucy, even,' Tessa murmured, and when he frowned and leaned forward to catch what she had said, she smiled brightly and nodded in the direction of her sister. 'I said, here's Lucy!'

Curtis felt another spark of intense irritation and the uncomfortable feeling that she was somehow getting away, though there was no reason to think that. He would corner her later on, somehow, but in the meantime he smiled as Lucy approached and pulled a low, fabric-covered stool next to them.

'I always wondered how Boxing Day things were conducted in the houses of the Great and Good,' she exclaimed, grinning and flopping down on the stool, which was so low that she had to stretch her legs out in front of her at an angle.

'The Great and Good. Hmm. Not sure too many of my family members would allow me into that particular club, but does it live up to expectations anyway?'

'An awful lot of hard work, from what I see. Don't you agree, Tess? I mean, on Boxing Day we normally run to a couple of people, left-over turkey sandwiches and drunken games of charades once we've polished off all the chocolates in the house.'

'Which just goes to show how far apart our worlds are, Luce!' It was an opportunity too good to pass up. The opportunity to project just the smallest of warnings to her sister that this man was definitely not all he cracked himself up to be. 'This is Curtis's reality, even though he does such a brilliant job at being one of the ordinary people!'

Lucy seemed stunned by this observation, but then giggled a little nervously. Curtis looked enraged. Quietly, darkly and silently enraged. Tessa smiled blandly at him, as though there were absolutely nothing wrong in stating the obvious.

She wondered whether she should push the boat out with another ingenuous observation, but those narrowed, furious eyes, so far from the teasing charm that came naturally to him, made her think again. She stood up and excused herself.

'I'm going to see if I can find your mum,' she said, scanning the room. 'If not, I think I'll corner Anna again. I'll leave you two to it. Oh, you can have a look at Lucy's portfolio! She said you were interested in some of the stuff that she was doing!' If the portfolio had been some kind of ruse, then too bad. Lucy would have to sit through an inspection and suffer any consequent embarrassment.

She saw them exchange a quick look and then Lucy hurried into speech, apologising in advance for the quality of her work but unable to suppress the excitement in her voice.

Tessa slowly walked off, head held high, feeling Curtis's eyes boring into her from behind.

If she could spend the remainder of the time avoiding him, then she would.

It largely worked out that way. His relatives were all highly sociable people and she found that her foot was an immediate ice-breaker with them. The fact that she worked for Curtis was a further source of conversation, most of it highly entertaining. And Isobel, busy and flustered, was a delight, since Tessa had only ever thought of her as the embodiment of elegance and calm. It was nice to see this big family group, with their long-time friends, enjoying the fact of being together.

From wherever she was in the room, she was aware of Curtis with Lucy, aware of his eyes following her, trying to puzzle out her mood, was even aware when they disappeared for a short while, Lucy with her portfolio under her arm.

She saw them slip away, towards the middle of the afternoon, just when the curtains were being drawn and coffee was being served with liqueurs. Her heart seemed to stop beating for a few seconds and she was aware of the catch in her throat as she continued to chat to Anna and Isobel, while her mind swelled with images of what they might be getting up to.

A quick, cursory flick through some pictures and then what…? A kiss? One of those hungry, urgent kisses that she herself had been a victim of? A kiss aimed at catapulting down any barriers? Not that there would be any barriers between them. Lucy wasn't a barrier kind of girl. Tessa didn't think there would be any angst-filled questions, any doubts. She had to force herself back into the conversation, but her body was taut when they eventually emerged, both talking urgently together, his dark head inclined to meet her fair one.

Curtis spotted her immediately. She was sitting down on one of the plump chairs, foot resting on a small, velvet-covered footstool, chatting to old Colonel Watson, one of his parents' friends. For a few seconds he just stared at her, drinking in that calm, serious expression as she listened to whatever George Watson was rambling on about. She had tucked her hair neatly behind her ears, but every time she moved her head some escaped and swished against her cheek and then she would automatically tuck it back into position.

Lucy had wandered off to play with the kids, and for a moment his eyes lingered between the two of them, musing on how physically different they were. Blonde and vivacious stacked against brunette and wary.

From across the room, Tessa caught that look as his eyes

followed Lucy thoughtfully. He was comparing them. She read that as clearly as if he had it written in large script across his forehead. Comparing and contrasting. Or perhaps just contrasting. She couldn't remember a time when she had been jealous of Lucy. Lucy was Lucy and her stream of boyfriends and adoring admirers had been a source of amusement for Tessa but nothing else. But now jealousy filled her like a poison and she closed her eyes for a few fleeting seconds. When she opened them it was to find that Curtis had bridged the space between them and was standing by her, gazing down from his great height.

'Oh!' Tessa said, flustered that she had been speculating about him and now here he was, as if he had read her thoughts and decided to wander over to find out more. 'You're back.'

'Back?'

'From having a look at Lucy's portfolio. What did you think of her work?' She turned to the colonel and began explaining what her sister did, taking much longer with the explanation than was necessary, just to garner some self-control, while Curtis stood and stared down at her.

The colonel made one or two jocular remarks about his lack of artistic talent, his admiration for anyone who knew what to do with some charcoal or a paintbrush, and then excused himself to check up on Isobel, make sure she hadn't collapsed from overexertion. Which left her all alone with Curtis.

He sat down in the colonel's chair. When he spoke, his voice was normal enough but his blue eyes were watchful and assessing. Assessing what? Assessing how she would react to his budding involvement with her sister? The sickening, faint feeling that had plagued her since she had first overheard that conversation was replaced by a dead, still, cold calm.

He was asking her something about whether she was having fun. Tessa nearly laughed aloud at that one.

'Absolutely,' she said neutrally. 'Your relatives are all so nice and it's great seeing Anna again. She looks wonderful.'

'In her twenty-first-century clothing.' Curtis grinned, trying unsuccessfully to drag her from her zoned-out state. 'I think she's done a ritual burning of the old-fashioned frocks and Alice bands.'

'She hasn't, has she?' Tessa gasped, momentarily distracted, and he laughed and touched her cheek with one brown finger.

'I hope not. Those clothes cost quite a bit. I've told her that the least she could do is give them to charity. I'm keeping my fingers crossed that she doesn't interpret that as free rein to go and buy whatever she wants in the expectation that I now have no right to object.'

Where he had touched her had left a hot, stinging trail. It was all she could do not to wipe it away with the back of her fist.

'I'm sure she's far too sensible to do that,' Tessa said obligingly, and he gave her another quick, frustrated look from under his lashes.

'Tessa, what's goi—'

'Lord, is that the time?' she interrupted quickly, before he could start on any difficult conversations. 'Work tomorrow. We really must go. I wonder if your mother needs any help with the clearing up?'

'No, she definitely doesn't need any help with any clearing up,' he grated, catching her by her wrist as she began to stand. 'She might insist on doing all the cooking but she does relent when it comes to the aftermath. She has people come in to do that for her. We've barely exchanged two words all day, do you realise that?'

'It's difficult at something like this,' Tessa said on a note of desperation. Caught in mid-motion, she didn't know whether to sit back down or wrestle her hand out of his vice-like grip. 'So many people around,' she elaborated vaguely.

'You should try my mother's New Year's Eve parties.' Curtis relaxed enough to grin. 'Always starts small, just a few close friends, and by the time December the thirty-first has come round, the few close friends has always managed to swell into eighty-odd and counting. We have to talk. There's something I need to tell you…' The grin got a little wider and Tessa felt panic hit her like a fist right in her stomach. She just knew, with sudden foreboding, that somewhere in his next sentence her sister's name would be mentioned.

'It's about Lucy…'

CHAPTER NINE

REFLECTING back, Tessa was amazed that those three little words, unintentionally aimed straight at her heart, hadn't resulted in an immediate breakdown. Right there, half standing, half sitting, with Curtis's firm hand closed over her wrist. In fact, her utter composure had been a great reminder to her that she would be able to get through this and put it behind her. An ability to keep up appearances was everything. After all, didn't you eventually believe the myths you started creating about yourself? Show the world that you were strong, that you hadn't been hurt, and sooner or later you would find yourself no longer having to pretend.

She had smiled brightly and exclaimed that there was no need to launch into this particular conversation about her sister, that she already knew. And then, when he had still been in his stunned phase, she had managed to release herself from his fingers and return to the noisy bustle of the party, where several people had conveniently been paying their respects to the hostess before taking their leave.

She and Lucy had managed to slip out before she could be cornered again by him and forced to hear the quiet letdown, the rueful sheepishness that her sister's attractions were just so much greater and more inviting. She had even managed to avoid the worst-case scenario, which was being asked, urgently and passionately, whether she would mind not saying anything about what they had got up to just in case it jeopardised his chances with her sister.

However, she had known what she had to do.

Nevertheless, she could feel a wave of nauseous nervousness sweep through her as she walked through the familiar doors of the office building.

The feeling intensified on the ride up, where she maintained a glassy-eyed, fixed stare in front of her, ignoring every other person in the lift.

She had decided to arrive as early as possible, in the hope that she would get to the office before him. Time for a strong cup of coffee and a few stern lectures to herself before she had to face the reality of his overwhelming presence.

As luck would have it, he was there. Tessa spotted him the minute she walked into her office, through the open door that led to his. He was sprawled back in his chair, legs propped up on the desk, surveying something on his computer. His jeans were faded to almost white in patches and he was wearing a long-sleeved black tee shirt. Conservative dressing by his standards and he looked shockingly sexy.

'God, you're early!' His eyes crinkled in an appreciative smile. 'Half the staff are off for a couple more days and the other half will be taking their time getting here.' He beckoned her with one finger and, though he was still smiling, his eyes were serious.

Just in case he was thinking of continuing the conversation he had been obliged to abort the evening before, Tessa rooted through her bag and carefully placed the envelope on the desk in front of him.

He looked at it for a few seconds, then said brusquely, 'What's this?'

'Open it and you'll find out. Can I get you some coffee?'

'No, you can stay right there until I see what you've given me.' He dropped his feet to the ground, leaned forward and took the envelope, opening it in one swift movement as he slid back into his reclining position.

Tessa didn't look at him as he read, and re-read and re-read again. She focused on her fingers instead, spread clammily on her skirt.

'It's a letter of resignation,' Curtis said eventually, his voice devoid of any intonation, and this time she did look at him. His lips were narrowed in a thin line and he was frowning, but not in a puzzled way. More in a savagely grim way.

'I know what it is. I wrote it.'

'Mind telling me why? Or do I have to guess?'

'Well, as I mentioned in the letter, the job is brilliant, but it's just not for me.'

'Why not?'

'We did say from the start that there would be a three-month probationary period,' Tessa hedged. 'You would be free to give me my walking papers if you didn't like what you got and I would be free to do the same.'

'And you've decided to go down that route even though you've spent, let's see now, eight lines extolling the fabulous nature of the work.' He leaned back, folded his hands behind his head and proceeded to give her the full benefit of his attention. It was like being hosed down in freezing water. His eyes were chips of ice.

In her head, Tessa had imagined that her resignation, after the first few platitudes of regret and maybe a token attempt to tempt her to stay, would be happily accepted. After all, wasn't she freeing him up to commence a full-blown affair with Lucy, without having her around like a guilty conscience draped round his neck?

She hadn't thought that she would have to account for her decision.

'Do you mind if I sit down?'

For a few seconds, he looked as though he might just insist that she remain standing, but eventually he nodded briefly at the chair in front of his desk and she sank into it with a feeling of relief.

'So…you were about to explain why you feel the need to leave this job even though…' he picked up the letter lying on his desk and quoted from it '"…It is enjoyable and invigorating and has provided an invaluable window of experience which will prove very influential when seeking a new position elsewhere…"'

'I just think…' What *did* she think? Quoting her own resignation letter back to her had been a dirty trick. Now she was supposed to come up with some plausible reason why she was quitting a supposed dream job. And she could hardly start waffling on about the money because the money was just another dreamy aspect of it.

'Cut the crap, Tessa. We both know why you've suddenly decided that you have to quit.'

Silence. Tessa cringed into her chair and stared firmly down at the tips of her shoes. So, she had managed to dodge the inevitable let-down chat the evening before and now she was going to have it drummed into her head.

She didn't notice him vacating his chair and wasn't aware of what he was doing until he was leaning right over her, hands gripping the sides of her chair, his face thrust aggressively close to hers.

'I just want to hear you say it,' he grated softly.

That did it. This time she looked him straight in the eye, her rising anger matching his own.

As if it wasn't enough that she knew what he was up to! Oh, no, he was determined to have it out in the open so that they could discuss it! Presumably like two adults. Maybe he needed to talk about it so that he could put any tiny speck of conscience he had to bed.

'Okay. I'm leaving because I know what's going on between you and my sister and I don't think it's appropriate for me to continue working for you under those circumstances.'

'You *know what's going on between me and your sister*?' Bafflement was quickly replaced by cold, dawning comprehension. Tessa wondered, for a few fleeting seconds, whether she might have made a mistake, but then decided that she had heard what she had heard, and, as if that weren't enough, she knew what she knew. That Lucy was his type. In Tessa's view, too many problems were caused by people trying to hide from the truth. She had seen enough of her friends and Lucy's to know that ignoring certain glaring facts always proved very costly emotionally. Woe betide the poor woman whose boyfriend started avoiding phone calls, when her response was to make excuses on his behalf instead of interpreting the situation the way it really was.

Their fling, if it even deserved to be in that category, had been, Tessa thought, fragile from the word go. He had never been going to hang about for very long and if she had made the fatal mistake of falling in love with him, then that was her fault and her fault alone.

'Care to elaborate?' There was a dangerous softness to his voice that she chose to ignore.

'I don't see the point of that. Would you mind moving? I can't breathe properly with you so close.'

He pushed himself away from her to go by the window where he proceeded to lean against the broad ledge, arms folded, like a judge contemplating a seriously irritating miscreant.

'You think…what *exactly*?'

'You know what I think! And there's no point trying to deny it. I heard the two of you whispering by the front door, discussing that perhaps it would be best to keep the situation from me. I heard! And, for heaven's sake, don't even try to patronise me by pretending that you don't have a clue what I'm talking about!'

'I wouldn't dream of patronising you and I remember the conversation distinctly.'

'Right. Good. In that case...' In that case, she thought, I'll just get my act together and leave.

'So in you jumped with your conclusions because, naturally, I'm the sort of bastard who sleeps with a woman and then has no compunctions about sharing himself with her sister. You wouldn't say that you know me better than that?'

'I never accused you of sleeping with Lucy,' Tessa mumbled uncomfortably.

'A minor technicality.' Curtis overrode her interruption coldly. 'Conspiring to meet up behind your back is as good as. And what a quick worker I am! Twenty minutes and I've already managed to make an assignation with a girl I didn't know from Adam! What a lot of faith you have in me! Not forgetting your sister, of course.'

'Lucy wouldn't have known about...about us...'

'Oh, that's all right, then. For her to arrange to meet me after a couple of minutes and some polite conversation. Does she normally do that sort of thing? Get involved with a perfect stranger without bothering with the niceties of getting to know him?'

'If you arranged to meet, then that would be step one in getting to know one another, wouldn't it?' Tessa shrugged. 'Hence my resignation. Working with you under those circumstances would be too uncomfortable. For both of us.'

'So, really, having written me off as a serial womaniser, you're doing the big-hearted thing and giving me the space to move on to another model without having to work with model number one.'

'That's about it.'

A deathly silence lengthened between them. Tessa could feel the vein in her neck pulsing and her heart hammering inside her like a steam engine.

'Fine.'

'I beg your pardon?'

'I said fine. You can go now. You're released from your employment with immediate effect. Any money the company owes you will be forwarded to your address and, naturally, I will provide a good reference for you when you find yourself another job.'

Tessa stared at him. She had got what she wanted. She was being released from the agony of working alongside him while he cavorted with her sister. In the long run, it had been the only option. Lucy might come and go in the blink of an eye, but there would be others, a long line of them. Fun-loving blondes, the sort he enjoyed having around brightening his office, the sort he enjoyed going out with. If she had stayed put, she would have had to endure each and every one and how thick could one person's skin be?

Logic and good, solid reason were no match for the awful loneliness spreading through her, though.

She made her legs move, made herself stand up and even propelled herself in the direction of him, stretching out her hand in the final, utterly polite, gesture of farewell.

Curtis looked at the outstretched hand with contempt.

'I don't think so,' he said icily.

Her hand dropped to her side and she felt tears well up and prick the backs of her eyes. That expression in his eyes was the very worst thing. It sliced right through her like a blade.

'I—' she began.

'Don't say a word,' he snarled. 'I think you've already said quite enough.' With that he spun round on his heel and stared out of the window, affording her the sight of his ramrod-straight back.

Let her go, Curtis thought savagely. He was aware of her hovering behind him, but there was no way he was going to rescue her from her self-inflicted discomfort. He continued to stare broodingly out of the window, not that there was much worth looking at. With spectacular predictability, it had failed to snow yet again and the skies were typically leaden. Everything looked monochrome and depressed.

He was aware of her departure with the sound of the door clicking shut, and only then did he slowly turn around and return to his chair, making no attempt to immerse himself in his work. He had no idea how long he sat there, staring at the wretched screen saver, while thoughts jostled in his head. He only knew that the next time he glanced out of the window, it had begun to snow. He guessed that all over London kids would be staring out of their windows in wonder, praying that the flurries would turn into something more substantial, something they could build a snowman out of. He had promised Anna that he would be home early, in time to take her and his mother out for an early supper somewhere. It had been his intention to invite Tessa along as well.

Clearly now out of the question.

He swivelled so that his chair was squarely facing the window and told himself that he had had a very lucky escape.

He had deviated from his usual course, had been blinded by a combination of seriousness, intelligence and humour, not realising that seriousness, intelligence and humour added up to a woman who would not be content to simply have a spot of fun.

Curtis frowned darkly at the window. He worked damned hard all year long. Relationships were about releasing him from the tensions of his job. Relationships were all about putting guilt-free fun into his life. They weren't about making him feel like this, feel like throwing things at the window and walking for hours in the snow because he needed to clear his head.

He swore softly and ineffectively under his breath, cursing the fact that there was no one in the office with whom he could indulge in some casual banter, just until his head got sorted. Flexitime had distinct drawbacks occasionally.

He slung his jumper on over the long-sleeved tee shirt, stuck on his coat and headed down, only remembering that his computer was still running when he was almost out of the office.

He wasn't too sure where he was heading. Only when he was outside, with the flakes gathering momentum around him and all trace of sun stifled under the thick grey skies, did he realise that he needed to see her.

She certainly didn't need to see him. In fact, Tessa thought as she turned the key to her front door, he was the last person in the world she ever wanted to clap eyes on again.

A tiny voice in her head pointed out that her wish had certainly been granted. He had made no move to stop her from leaving the company. A careless shrug had been all she had been worth at the end of the day. He hadn't even mentioned what they had had together. It had been so meaningless to him that he couldn't even be bothered to bring the subject up.

She dashed a couple of wayward tears from her eyes and pushed open the door.

Of course, just when she wanted to be on her own, Lucy was in. She could hear her sister clattering around in the kitchen, and, knowing that she could hardly avoid her, Tessa removed her coat, hung it on the coat stand by the door and reluctantly made her way to the origin of the noise.

'Would you believe it's snowing?' Lucy greeted her triumphantly, as though the fall of snow were something she had personally been involved in. As an afterthought, she added, frowning, 'Why are you home, anyway? I thought you'd gone off to work?'

Tessa sighed and sat down. 'Long story.'

'Will it be one of those long stories that I'll want to hear?' Lucy flopped into the chair facing hers and looked at Tessa with concern. 'You didn't have a relapse of your twisted-foot syndrome, did you?'

'Oh, no. Foot's fine.' It's the heart that's not doing too good, she added silently to herself. 'But, as of this moment, I'm officially on the dole.'

Lucy gaped. For a few seconds, Tessa forgot her worries and actually laughed because it took a lot to reduce her sister to speechlessness.

'You're joking!' Lucy searched her face for some semblance of humour, found none and sank back into her chair. 'Oh, my God, *why*?'

'Oh, you know. Not the job for me.'

'But...I thought you enjoyed working there. You told me that it was a lot more fun than your last place, that fuddy-duddy accountancy firm...I don't understand...'

Now came the careful tiptoeing-round-the-minefield part. To put off the dire moment, Tessa asked whether she could possibly have a cup of tea, and then thought about her next approach, while Lucy gabbled away in the background, expressing curiosity and surprise at the same time. Finally, mug in hand, she plonked it in front of her sister and said sternly, 'You've made a huge mistake. You had an invigorating, well-paid job and Curtis Diaz was most probably the best boss you could ever hope to find.'

'Curtis Diaz is a workaholic and a womaniser.'

'That doesn't make sense. Workaholics don't have time to womanise and, anyway, what do his private habits have to do with how much you enjoy your work?'

'Stop quizzing me about this, Luce,' Tessa said irritably. 'I'm tired and I have another headache. I don't need you to start playing older sis with me.'

'Because you think you've monopolised that position!' Lucy retorted quick as a flash. 'Well, I just want to tell you that quitting your job has really jeopardised things for me. I mean, did Curtis mention anything about me? No, I don't suppose he would have. If he knew that you'd made your mind up, he wouldn't have wanted to put you under any pressure to stay. Mind you...' she stared off into the distance, oblivious to Tessa '...there's no real reason why everything should come to a halt just because you've suddenly decided that you hate working for him...'

'Lucy, *what are you on about*?'

'I mean...he really *did* like what he saw yesterday. I know he did. He *said* he did, but I just get the feeling that he's not one of those guys who says something just for the sake of it...do you?'

'Liked *what*?' This conversation was getting surreal. What had Curtis seen that he had liked? Had they been playing some kind of adult doctor-and-nurse game for the half an hour that they'd been closeted away in his mother's house? Surely they couldn't have been that overcome with lust? A sick feeling clawed away at her stomach, threatening to make her bring up the few mouthfuls of tea she had just swallowed.

'Well...we were going to tell you this together but...' She couldn't help it. She smiled. A broad, thrilled smile that lit up her face. 'God, Tess, it's the most exciting thing ever!'

Tessa could think of nothing to say. Her throat had closed up and really she doubted whether she would have been able to speak even if she had wanted to. The truth was going to come at her from every angle, she now realised. It didn't matter how much she tried to deflect the blows, they would still come because they would never be able to keep a relationship between them silent.

'You know when Curtis came round the other evening...Lord, but it feels like a thousand years ago!' Her eyes sparkled as she leant forward, propping her chin in her hand. She had wonderful, tumbling hair that she occasionally straightened, when she wanted to look glamorous. Now, it was a riotous jumble of curls cascading past her shoulders.

'Yes, I remember.' Tessa sighed quietly.

'Well, he asked me all about what I was doing at college and then he told me that I might be just the person to work on some logos for him. You know he's thinking about extending parts of his operation to the Far East...'

What she was hearing seemed to be coming at her from a long way off. In fact, it took a few seconds for it to sink in, then she said, on a whisper, 'What are you talking about, Luce?'

'My work! What else? We decided not to say anything to you because I know you. I knew you'd be disappointed if you thought that I'd been rejected, but yesterday, after he had a look at my portfolio, he said that he was prepared to give me a stab at it. He was so sweet about it! Not patronising at all. He said he liked my work, that it was quirky and inventive, which would be just the sort of thing he would be looking for…'

'Your work…' Tessa said hollowly.

'Why aren't you excited?' Lucy demanded, pausing in her breathless excitement to realise that the expected reaction had not arrived.

'I am. Excited and thrilled.' Tessa forced herself to smile but the smile was strained. Why hadn't he said anything? Why hang on to his silence, letting her fling herself into accusations that were wildly off target?

She remember the puzzled look on his face when she had informed him that she knew about his feelings for her sister.

'What about your course?' she asked faintly, dragging the subject back to the prosaic and leaving her restless mind free to wander unimpeded. 'You can't possibly give that up. Not when you've come so far…'

But Lucy had everything sorted and Tessa half listened, only stirring herself when mention was made of food and, buoyed up by the prospect of her first successful dip into the brave world of advertising, Lucy actually volunteered to go out and buy some. With her own money.

Once she was gone, Tessa went into the sitting room and just let the sound of silence drift over her. Peaceful though it was, it wasn't nearly peaceful enough to end the nasty tangle of thoughts writhing around in her head like hungry serpents. She moaned softly and closed her eyes.

She still had them optimistically closed when the doorbell went.

The prospect of lunch, even though it might be procured and prepared by her sister in a very rare excursion into domesticity, did not appeal. Tessa didn't feel hungry. In fact, she felt as though she had crashed headlong into a brick wall.

Which was *good*, she told herself, trundling to the front door. Because, face it, even if things hadn't gone utterly pear-shaped now, they would have further down the line. She and the brick wall would *still* have become close acquaintances somewhere in the future.

She pulled open the front door and her eyes travelled up, and up, and up until they finally rested on Curtis's dark, glowering face. At which point something like electricity shot through her veins, making her take a step backwards from the impact.

In that brief instant of stunned hesitation, Curtis pushed his way inside and slammed the door shut behind him, then he leaned heavily against it and stared down at her.

'What are you doing here?' Tessa asked in a small voice. She took a few more steps backwards, putting distance between them. Her hands fluttered nervously and she clasped them together in front of her.

'Just passing by. Thought I'd drop in. About now, you should start hurling more accusations about me and your sister, wouldn't you say? Something along the lines of what a bastard I am?'

'You should have told me.'

'Told you what.'

'That I was wrong about you and Lucy. That you were interested in her work. That that was what all the hushed voices were all about, as well as her desperation to get to your mother's Boxing Day do. Because she wanted to show you her portfolio. I shouldn't have had to hear it all from my sister.'

'And what…stop you in mid-rant?' He had spent the last hour cooling his heels at his usual coffee shop close to the office, giving his composure time to return to working condition. In fact, he had never had so many about-turns in his life before. One minute he had wanted to storm over to her place and give her a piece of his mind, because why the hell should he allow her to drag his reputation into the mud without murmuring a single word of protest? The next minute, he was telling himself that she wasn't worth the effort of an argument, that she could think precisely what she wanted and the fact that he knew the truth was enough.

In fact, he had worked his way through two espressos and a bacon roll before coming to the decision that he was a man of honour and, as such, had a right to put her straight on one or two of her assumptions.

In a very cool, very detached, laudably rational way, of course. After all, all he would be doing would be to put her straight and move on with a clean slate. Get right back to the sort of woman he understood. Some uncomplicated, fun creature. The world was full of them, as he had always found.

Looking at this particular woman now, though, was doing nothing for all his good intentions. He didn't feel very cool or detached or even rational, come to think of it.

'No,' he drawled, moving towards her until they were doing a weird dance, with Tessa retreating in the face of Curtis's slow, relentless advance. 'How cruel would I have been not to have allowed you the pleasure of ripping my personality to shreds?'

'I didn't rip your personality to shreds,' Tessa mumbled, wincing. She had now backed herself into the sitting room and she scuttled into the closest chair, curling into it.

'No?' Curtis intoned silkily. He was no longer advancing on her, but, almost as bad, prowling through the room like a great jungle cat exploring the limits of its cage. And he was every bit as threatening as any great jungle cat. 'If I remember accurately, you accused me of seducing your sister in this very house, when I was still fresh from sleeping with *you*, of arranging to meet her with your smell still lingering in my nostrils. Now, I'm not sure what school of morality you attended, but the one I went to clearly stated that those types of accusations come into the category of *personality shredding*!' Each sibilant, vicious word was like a drop of poison.

He had ceased his restless prowling and was now standing in front of her, hands shoved into his trouser pockets, his face a mask of freezing contempt.

'You should have said something,' Tessa flung at him. She lifted her chin and eyed him mutinously. 'You let me jump to all the wrong conclusions and now you think you can just walk in and throw it in my face!'

Had he thought for one minute, seriously, that she would open the door, meekly and tearfully accept what he had to say, fall at his feet with hands clasped in apology, simply because she had made a mistake? Her cheeks were two burning patches of colour and the stubborn tilt of her chin spoke volumes for her determination to fight him right back.

Let her.

Yes. Yes, he had done the right thing in coming here. Every muscle in his body was pulsing and it was a damn sight healthier than that impotent, frustrated, dead feeling he had had earlier.

And he still wanted her. With all her complications, her intolerance of his basic ground rule of *just have fun*, her wild accusations. A sex thing. But he felt his rage ratchet up a notch and this time it was directed solely at himself.

He angrily stalked off and sat down, glowering. 'I was going to let you walk away. Of course I knew you'd find out the truth sooner or later, but guess what? Why should I drop it? Why should I allow you to get away with defamation of my character? I notice you haven't even had the common decency to *apologise*!'

'Okay. I'm sorry. I'm *sorry.* I jumped to the wrong conclusions. Satisfied?'

'Not really, no.'

'Because…?'

'Because it's more than just jumping to the wrong conclusions, isn't it? It's about trust. What kind of man do you think I am? That's the basic question, isn't it?'

'What was I supposed to think?'

'You were supposed to think that a few overheard snatches of conversation just might not add up to the worst possible conclusion. You were *supposed to think* that you knew me well enough to presume me innocent before condemning me to the guillotine.' He knew how he sounded. Cold, indifferent, composed. He knew that only he would be able to discern the awful truth behind what he was saying, which was that he had been hurt. Curtis Diaz, the man who had always burnt the candle at both ends, the man who worked hard and played hard, had been hurt.

Tessa's face was closed as she looked at him. Now *this* argument, she thought, was one she could really get her teeth into. He obviously hadn't followed through with his logic. Unusual for him, since he had the most logical brain of any man she had ever met, but everyone had a blind spot and this was his. He was a charming, dangerously sexy man who nurtured a reputation for never staying with one woman for too long, whose tastes had always run to a very specialised type of female, and yet he naively thought that he should be seen as Mr Trustworthy. The ego of the man!

Tessa focused very hard on that side of him. The side that wasn't witty and thoughtful and sharp and ironic. She concentrated on his house-sized ego. Safer.

'Why do you think I should have done that?' she asked, with a coldness that almost matched his but didn't quite. 'Why do you think I should have heard what sounded like a very compromising conversation and immediately come to the conclusion that it was innocent?' She would have done, she knew it, if she'd thought that he loved her, because mutual love was all about trust. But she was just a passing fancy and passing fancies didn't necessarily qualify for exclusivity. That was life.

'Look at you!' Tessa continued, gathering momentum as her heart protected itself by projecting a one-dimensional cardboard cut-out image of him. 'You're not exactly noted for your celibate nature...'

'Meaning that I see nothing wrong in overlapping relationships?'

'I never said that you would have gone out with Lucy while I was still trailing in the background like some inconvenient unfinished business. But you're not exactly the solid type who places a whole lot of emphasis on cultivating long-standing relationships, are you?'

'Why did you sleep with me if I didn't fit into that niche?'

'Because...' Tessa glared back at him, carelessly lounging there in the chair as if he had a perfect right to be there.

'You're upset because you thought that I had lived down to my reputation. Upset enough to quit a job you loved doing. But when we went to bed together, I was still that man, so why did you decide to come to bed with me? Were you hoping that somehow I'd change? That you'd be able to turn me into a domestic dream who wanted nothing more than to slip into commitment and live happily ever after with a few kiddies running around and a dog in front of the Aga?'

CHAPTER TEN

'I THINK it's time you left.' Tessa got to her feet with as much dignity as she could muster. Curtis's question had shaken her to the core. How could she have thought for a minute that his lessons in logic might have been incomplete? With a few short observations, he had stripped her reaction down to the bone. What she didn't want to do was give him any opportunity to go further.

'I'm not ready to leave.' And he wasn't. He really wasn't. Because he was back in the driving seat, utterly and totally in control. When he left, he would have put her straight on her vast misconception of his character. He wasn't a commitment guy. That was for his brother, who loved the routine and order of his life. He, himself, had never cared for routine. His job predicated against any sort of routine, anyway. That had been the beauty of his wife, when she was alive. She too had been full of the joy of living and pregnancy had not really interfered with that.

His only grounding now came from being a father. For Anna he would take time off work, for Anna he would postpone meetings and attend school concerts whenever he could. But that was it. Absolutely. The thought of having some wife in the background nagging about his hours and reminding him of deadly dinner parties she had arranged for the weekend was just not on his agenda.

'Since you happen to be in *my* house, whether or not you're ready to go isn't the point. The point is I want you out. You've got your apology and now we have nothing left to say.' Her breath caught in her throat at that. The house-sized ego she had been focusing so intently on vanished like a puff of smoke. All she thought was, You were such fun, you could make me laugh and make me abandon every ounce of common sense just to feel you close to me. You could make me love you.

The dangerous thoughts crept into her head like thieves, stealing her will-power.

'You haven't answered my question,' Curtis said, not budging. 'And you might as well sit back down. I'm not ready to leave, not yet, and I don't see how you can force me out. I'm all for equality of the sexes, but when it comes to physical strength, we're still poles apart.'

'Oh, right! When in doubt, just fall back on the caveman principle, why don't you?'

'Answer my question and I'll go.'

Tessa sat back down, furious and helpless at the same time. 'I never saw you as relationship potential,' she spat out. 'Never.'

'Then I expect you'll be wanting your job back, in that case? Now that we've established that there's nothing going on between me and your sister?'

'And slide back into being your casual fling till you get bored of me? No, thanks!' The words were out before she could take them back, and they flew through the sudden, thick silence with the efficiency of the contents from Pandora's box. Tessa could feel the blood rush to her face and she had to stop herself from groaning out loud. Everything she had been trying so hard to deny was wrapped up in those few careless words and he knew it. She could see it on his face.

'Because that wouldn't be enough for you, would it?' Curtis said softly. 'You're just not the type of woman who can have flings.'

Tessa hoped he wasn't expecting an answer to that because he wasn't going to get one. She would just have to let him spin his yarn and then he would leave. His life would carry on its own merry way and she would pick up the pieces and start again.

'I'm sorry,' he said. Horribly, he sounded as if he meant it. Tessa cringed inwardly and wished she could somehow magic herself out of the room, out of the house, maybe even out of the country. Anywhere she could escape to where those piercing blue eyes couldn't bore into her soul and read what was written there.

'I don't want commitment. Not yet. Maybe not ever.' He stood up slowly. 'I don't get turned on by the prospect of shopping for rings or by the thought of coming back home to the smell of home-cooked food.'

He had an image of her, waiting for him at the end of the day, smiling when he walked through the door, asking him how his day had been.

'I don't need anyone asking me how my day went,' he ground out more forcefully than he had intended. 'Aren't you going to say anything?' he snapped, angry with her because somehow she had made him think thoughts he had no business thinking.

'What's there to say?' Tessa asked wearily. 'You're right. I'm not a casual kind of girl and I never could be. I was stupid to ever have gone to bed with you, but we all make mistakes.'

Curtis didn't much care for being called a mistake. Why, he didn't know.

'I thought I could just have fun, but I was wrong. I knew that when Lucy appeared on the scene and I thought you were interested in her.'

'You were jealous, in other words.' That was much better. He really rather liked the idea of Tessa being jealous. More than liked it. It made his heart sing crazily. What man's heart wouldn't? he thought to himself. Perfectly normal human reaction.

'I was realistic,' Tessa corrected coldly. 'You've chosen the road you want to go down, and good luck to you. It's not the road I want and I don't intend wasting time indulging in something that's going nowhere.'

'I couldn't agree more.' Curtis moved towards the door, waiting for her to stand up to see him out, which he soon realised she had no intention of doing, although she wanted him out. That was pretty clear from the shuttered, cool expression on her face. 'I don't personally see it as wasting time, but there you go. Different strokes for different folks.'

'That's right.'

He hesitated, wanting to ask her about her foot but knowing that that was stupid when they had just waged World War III, bar the shooting. 'Tell Lucy to get in touch with me so that we can formally discuss details of this job. And tell her to make sure that her passport's up to date. She might need to fly out to one or two proposed sites at short notice.'

'Sure.' Tessa looked at him, taking him in for the last time.

'You can come in with her and collect your pay-cheque,' Curtis heard himself say. His face darkened at the sudden crack in his armour but if she noticed anything, she didn't show it.

'I'd rather you posted it to me.'

'Look, we're adults. There's no need for you to avoid me like the plague. Chances are that we'll even bump into one another in the course of things, if Lucy takes on the commission and things go according to plan...'

The thought of *bumping into him* was enough to make her feel sick. Since when did convalescents expose themselves witlessly to the cause of their illness?

'I don't see any reason why we should meet again. And I'd really rather Personnel posted the cheque to me. I'm going to be out and about looking for a job. I can't guarantee that I'll be able to pop in at the drop of a hat.'

'Sure. Well, whatever.'

'Just slam the door behind you. It self-locks.' With that, she turned away, dismissing him.

Suited him just fine, Curtis decided, striding out of the room and slamming the front door behind him.

It had all gone according to plan. Really. He had come to state his case and state it he had. What she had said had only confirmed his suspicions that she had been a dangerous near miss. She had wanted more and she had told him so in no uncertain terms. He was a free man. He would spend the rest of the school holidays juggling his work so he could take Anna out, maybe even buy her some new clothes in the sales, before she went back to school. He thought back to that day when his daughter and Tessa had gone shopping, the glow of achievement on her face. Well, he didn't think he would be able to match that as far as shopping partners went, but so be it.

It would be his first step in getting his life back to normal, back where he wanted it to be, where he was in control. Leave the unpredictability for his job.

He drove to his mother's house, having originally planned to return to the office where he would be able to submerge himself in work. In his head he played out the conversation he had just had with Tessa. He didn't want to. What he wanted was to now wash his hands of her altogether. But his mind was refusing to co-operate.

He had done what he had set out to do. That was good. Leaving her with the impression that he had somehow, ludicrously, managed to get involved with her sister was a misconception he hadn't been able to ignore in the end and he had sorted that out.

Frowning as his logical brain backtracked and fitted pieces together, he very nearly went into the back of someone at some traffic lights that had turned red. A minor interruption to his concentration. There was some link he should be making, he thought restlessly, some vital connection, and then as his car purred away at the traffic lights it happened and it was like being catapulted into the air at full speed.

Tessa was a commitment girl. She had said so herself. What she had failed to mention was what he was now figuring out for himself.

Commitment girls would never get involved with a man purely because it promised to be a spot of fun, no matter how powerful the attraction might be. He knew that in the depth of his bones and from the very summit of his experience. Women who seriously sought commitment wouldn't even be *attracted* to a man like him. They might look, but they would never venture near.

Which meant that Tessa had become involved because… because…

The conclusion that he had been inexorably working towards now presented itself to him. She had fallen in love with him. Maybe she didn't realise it herself, maybe she was just pretending to herself that, really, it had all been fun and she had got out before it was too late, but he thought otherwise. He thought that she had fallen in love with him even before she had slept with him and, subconsciously, her physical capitulation had just been the logical consequence of her emotional involvement.

He found that he was driving on automatic, not even realising where he was going, and was startled when his car suddenly appeared to be at his mother's place. His head felt fuzzy, almost as though important brain connections had been subtly altered so that his responses weren't what they should be. Everything was just a bit off kilter. And there was a pounding rush deep inside him, which he couldn't understand or deal with. He just knew one thing. His narrow escape must have been a hell of a lot narrower than he had imagined. He felt as though he had been too close to a fire and had been singed.

Singed but not burnt. Lucky him. And tomorrow he would probably be fully healed and ready to move forward. He would have her out of his head. In a week's time, he might even be seeing someone else, someone uncomplicated, straightforward and up for some fun, no strings attached…

A mere three days later, when Tessa spotted him in the gossip column of the newspaper, cavorting with a blonde, she made her mind up. She needed a break. The thought of seeing the new year in with Lucy around, puzzled and curious and waiting for the right time to launch into a detailed interrogation, just wouldn't do. Nor would the inevitable sleepless night, heady fuzzy with thoughts of him kissing the blonde as the clock struck twelve.

She had to get away, right away. Be on her own in different surroundings. The familiarity of the house stirred up too many painful memories. The four walls were no longer her haven but her torture chamber, impregnated with his dynamic, restless personality, and she needed time out from it.

She didn't even bother to tell her sister face to face. She couldn't face the concern and the questions.

So she left a note on the kitchen table. She would be in Dublin. She gave the name of the hotel and the phone number in case of an emergency, but failed to mention when she would be back.

And it felt glorious to walk out of the house, with a holdall, two good books and no one asking her what she was doing.

The feeling persisted on the flight over, and even the reality of checking into the hotel wasn't sufficient for Tessa to doubt for a single minute that she had done the right thing.

The place she had managed to find so close to New Year was small and cosy. She took a deep breath and filled her nostrils with the fragrant scent of polished wood and lavender. There were intimate touches everywhere, from the pretty furnishings to the pictures on the walls. She would shop during the day and then just read in the com munal, oak-panelled sitting room with the roaring fire and clumps of deep, worn chairs. Read and forget. She could feel herself forgetting already!

It was a mantra she kept up for the remainder of the day, which was spent browsing in the shops, having lunch in a café where she watched the world hurry by under brilliant blue but freezing skies, and reading book number one in front of the fire. The couple who ran the tiny hotel were charming and showed no curiosity at her request to eat early so that she could retire to her room before midnight. By dinnertime, as she was ushered to a small table at the back of the discreetly lit dining room, now festive in preparation for celebrations later, Tessa was convinced that she was finally beginning to unwind. Maybe, she considered lazily, she would move to Dublin permanently. Start afresh. Forget everything and most of all forget Curtis Diaz.

Which was why, taking her time with her soup and letting her mind toy with the fantasy of a time ahead when she could barely remember his name, let alone what he looked like, Tessa almost managed not to see the tall, dark figure that was suddenly looming at the far end of the room. He was talking to Bill Winters, the owner of the hotel while his eyes drifted slowly across the expanse of the dining area. And those blue eyes connected with hers just as realisation hit home with a resounding crash. Even so, the sight of Curtis *here* was sufficiently unbelievable for her to take it in. So she watched as he crossed the room, blinking in disbelief. The vision didn't clear. It continued to come closer until her shocked brain forced her to acknowledge that this was no dream. Curtis Diaz was here. At which point she gently returned her soup spoon to its bowl, before it clattered to the floor, and eyed him with gaping horror.

'Your sister told me where you were,' he said heavily. 'Carry on eating. I don't want to disrupt your meal.'

Disrupt her meal? What about disrupting her life? He had no right to be here, Tessa thought with uncurling anger. He had no right to just show up when she was trying so hard to forget all about him!

'I seem to have lost my appetite.' He was staring at her and she couldn't fathom what was in those dangerous, deep blue eyes. 'Why have you come here?' she demanded in a low, shaking voice. 'It's New Year's Eve…shouldn't you be out somewhere?' *With a leggy blonde?*

'Do you think I want to be here?' Curtis rasped, raking his fingers through his hair. 'I came because I had to.'

Which smelled to Tessa of work. Curtis Diaz only felt obligated to do things that impacted on his professional life. Mr No Commitment had no such qualms when it came to emotions, she thought bitterly.

'If it's to do with work, forget it. My replacement can deal with whatever I left behind. There's no way I'm going back to hold anyone's hand and walk them through my filing system.'

'It's not to do with work, for God's sake!' He banged one fist on the table and Tessa started back in alarm, heart beating like a sledgehammer.

'Then what? We've talked already. Too much. There's nothing left to say.'

'You never told me that you loved me.'

His words dropped like lead pellets into the thick pool of silence and every ripple that spread outwards was more horrifying than the last. Tessa felt her face whiten. She opened her mouth to speak and nothing came out.

'I...I...well,' she finally managed to say in a voice she didn't recognise as her own, 'I didn't because it's a ridiculous idea.' As if to lend edge to what she had said, she laughed hysterically, a little too hysterically.

Someone came to remove her soup bowl and she was aware of Curtis telling him to wait a while before he brought the next course. The instruction was accepted with a deferential nod. Tessa watched all this through a haze of sickening panic.

'It's not a ridiculous idea,' Curtis said quietly, leaning forward so that his elbows were on the table and the space between them was diminished to suffocating proportions. 'You're not the kind of girl to sleep with a man for no better reason than she wants to test the water or have a bit of fun. You're the kind of girl who sleeps with a man because she's involved with him, because her heart tells her it's the right thing to do.'

'I thought we'd established that,' Tessa muttered uncomfortably. 'Which is why I wasn't interested in a fling with you...'

'We established *that*,' Curtis agreed. 'Which made me wonder why you slept with me in the first place...'

Tessa's struggle to deny the truth collapsed. And she didn't even feel angry with him any more. She still wondered what he had had to gain by coming here, by cornering her, but even that curiosity was a pale shadow compared to her own sense of utter defeat.

'You're right,' she said. 'Did you think that this would be unfinished business unless you happened to drag the whole truth out of me?' She gave a short, mirthless laugh, but her eyes stung from the pressure of unshed tears and her fingers were compulsively twisting the serviette on her lap. 'Well, we wouldn't want that, would we? After all, Curtis Diaz is a man who *always* finishes business, isn't he? Even though this could have waited! So I'll help you out here. Yes. I didn't mean to and I knew that it was stupid, but once your heart starts galloping down a certain path, then it's impossible to catch up with it. I fell in love with you. Against all my better judgement, I fell in love with you and you're absolutely right. That's why I slept with you, because it just felt right. My only saving grace was that I knew from the word go that you weren't looking for a relationship. But I stupidly thought that maybe I *could* just enjoy something temporary. Thinking that you and Lucy were going to become an item made me realise that I couldn't. So, there you go, Curtis. Happy?'

'Amazingly, wondrously, fabulously happy.' He sent her a slow smile that made her toes curl and her mouth tighten.

'Good. I'm so glad for you. And now you've got that confession out of me, why don't you do me a huge favour and leave? Let me ring in the new year without you around to spoil it for me!'

'You seem to make a habit of asking me to leave when I don't want to.' He reached out and stroked her cheek before she had time to pull back. Now, it wasn't just her toes that were curling, but everything inside her as well.

'Do you really think that I just came here because I wanted the satisfaction of hearing you tell me?'

Tessa gave an eloquent shrug. Where he had touched her cheek burnt as though he had branded her.

'I came here because...' A dark flush spread across his cheekbones and he suddenly looked vulnerable and uncertain, two traits not normally associated with him.

'Because...?' Tessa prompted out of hateful, treacherous curiosity, when he lapsed into silence.

He met her eyes quickly and gave a slight shrug. 'Because I was that man. The one you described. The one who never wanted to put roots down. I felt that I had all the roots I needed with Anna and, besides, work never left time to cultivate anything, not that I couldn't have made the time if I'd wanted, but I didn't. I liked the life I had, or at least I thought I did.'

Tessa felt her breath catch in her throat. She didn't want hope to interfere with reality but the way he was looking at her...

'As you said, different strokes for different folks,' she said neutrally.

His hand reached out to cover hers, though, and she didn't remove it. The pressure of his palm against hers was warm and still and strong and as seductive as she remembered. Everything about him was.

'And I thought I meant it at the time, I really did.'

Tessa opened her mouth to speak and he briefly placed one finger over her lips.

'In fact, I told myself a lot of things a couple of days back, including that I was relieved to have escaped the possibility of getting caught up in a relationship I couldn't handle...no, wait, let me finish. I figured that I could walk away, breathe a sigh of relief, and get back to my life. I've been trying as hard as I could...'

'I know. I saw the picture in the newspaper of you trying with a blonde.'

Curtis snorted. 'I think *trying* would certainly be the word she would use to describe me. God, I can't even remember her name. She was just part of my Master Plan to get my life back and, in all fairness, she didn't mind being photographed with me. Upped her credibility in the world of glamour.'

He couldn't remember her name! Tessa's heart flipped a few times and reality gave up trying to put the dampener on hope.

'All I've succeeded in doing is drinking more than I should, storming around the office like a bear with a sore head, bellowing at anyone who crosses my path, not that I've had much of an audience, thank God, and staring at computer screens without managing to achieve very much.'

'Oh, I see,' Tessa said weakly.

'Do you? Can you? See, I mean? How much I missed you? I don't think you can. If someone had told me six months ago that I'd be running towards commitment as if my life depended on it, I'd have laughed them out of court.'

'You're saying…'

'I'm saying that…' He looked around uncomfortably and cleared his throat. 'I'm saying that I love you. Not just lust after you, although I do that as well, excel at it in fact, but need you and want you and can't bear the thought of you not being by my side. In fact…'

Their eyes tangled and Tessa smiled slowly back at him, reading his mind. 'I don't think anyone would miss us if we had a bit of a breather before the main course…'

They slunk out of the dining room like two teenagers, with Curtis just about managing to mutter something to their host on the way out about needing to fetch something before they carried on with the meal, that they would be back very shortly.

'Very shortly?' Tessa quizzed, half running up the stairs with him to her bedroom.

'Oh, yes. Remember what I said about lusting after you...? Well, it feels as though it's been years and I don't think my body is capable of behaving itself properly right now...' To demonstrate exactly what he meant, as soon as the key turned in the door he pushed it open and pulled her to him with a low groan, pressing her against the door to shut it, muttering thickly against her pliant mouth.

And his urgency matched hers. Hands collided as they tugged to free each other of unwanted clothes. Actually making it to the bed was not an option. 'We can spend all the time we want in bed later,' he promised roughly, 'but I want you right here and right now...'

With perfect understanding and feeling shockingly debauched, Tessa coiled her hands around his neck and groaned as their bodies found the perfect position. Her legs wrapped round him and, with a gasp of absolute fulfilment, she felt him move strongly inside her, thrusting and manoeuvring her with expertise so that her breasts bounced against his chest.

They came as one, shuddering on that final thrust, and Tessa curved lovingly against him as he carried her to the bed.

'Next time, my darling, we'll take all the time in the world, but I just couldn't wait...'

'Nor could I...' she murmured. She ran the palm of her hand against his chest and, with a smile, he did the same to her, pausing to cup her swollen breast in his hand and eliciting a tiny moan when he began rubbing her stiffened nipple between his fingers.

'You're the most beautiful creature on the face of the earth,' he said solemnly. 'Next to you, every woman seems to fade into the background.' As if unable to help himself, he lowered his head so that he could take one nipple into his mouth and suckle on it and Tessa was more than content to let him stay there, feasting, with her hand resting lightly on his head. She smiled when he finally looked up at her.

'My life only has meaning with you in it,' he told her, and she tugged him up so that their faces were once more on a level and she could gently kiss his mouth, pressing her body against his and moving sinuously against his already stiffening member.

'You don't know how I've longed to hear you say that,' she confessed, smiling and arching back as his hand curved along her thigh, seeking and finding the wetness that spoke of her desire. She drew her breath in sharply as his fingers rubbed insistently, sending shooting stars through her. 'What about the meal waiting downstairs?' She giggled, moving against his hand and then, reaching down, guiding his hardness against her sensitised softness.

'Mmm. Good question.' He grinned and rotated the tiny bud of femininity, loving the way she squirmed in response. 'I just had to touch you, Tessa...had to tell you how much I love you...how much I'm committed to a lifetime with you. I want you to have my kids, brothers or sisters for Anna, and I want you to grow old with me. And, yes, I really want you to ask me how my day went when I get back from work and arrange dinner parties with people when I'd rather just stay in and have a meal with you.'

'You mean with me and Anna and all those babies you want us to have...' How was it possible that she wanted to laugh and cry at the same time?

'That's right, my darling. The old year is on its way out, just like my old life is. The significance of the timing wasn't lost on me as I pulled out all the stops to get here, to see you. The end of something and the beginning of something else, something wonderful. For ever is in front of us…and it's perfect…'

'Yes,' Tessa breathed. 'Isn't it?'

'So what do we do? Go back down or just stay up here…?'

'Go back down, I think…' She smiled at him lovingly. 'But now I don't think I'll be coming up to my room to avoid the midnight hour…'

Was it her imagination or did Bill and his wife exchange a look of satisfaction when she told them that dinner would now be for two and that they would both be enjoying the celebrations together?

It didn't matter. All that mattered was that the man she loved was by her side and when the clock struck twelve, the lips that touched her own promised a future she had never dared dream of…

THE VENGEANCE AFFAIR *by Carole Mortimer*

Beau Garrett moved to the village of Aberton for a more peaceful life. But he became the target of gossip when he employed female gardener Jaz Logan. Soon he acted on his attraction to Jaz – and that's when the poison pen letters started arriving…

THE BILLION-DOLLAR BRIDE *by Kay Thorpe*

Gina Saxton has been left half of the Harlow billion-dollar empire – but there is a major condition: she must marry the heir to the other half, arrogant Ross Harlow! It's easy – until Gina realises that she's falling in love with her convenient husband!

THE MILLIONAIRE BOSS'S MISTRESS *by Madeleine Ker*

Anton Zell, a top entrepreneur, needs a PA to be at his side night and day. Amy Worthington takes on the challenge. But she's determined not to become just another notch on her gorgeous boss's bedpost – no matter how hard he tries to seduce her…

THEIR SCANDALOUS AFFAIR *by Catherine George*

Beautiful but fiery Avery Crawford wants her affair with Jonas Mercer to remain private, but the handsome millionaire wants their relationship to go public, and he's determined to marry Avery. However, Avery has secrets that come at a cost even Jonas can't afford…

Don't miss out…

On sale 4th February 2005

Available at most branches of WHSmith, Tesco, ASDA, Martins, Borders, Eason, Sainsbury's and all good paperback bookshops.

Visit www.millsandboon.co.uk